Stories
of Happy People

Also by Lars Gustafsson

The Death of a Beekeeper
(Translated by Janet K. Swaffar
and Gustram H. Weber)

The Tennis Players
(Translated by Yvonne L. Sandstroem)

Sigismund
(Translated by John Weinstock)

LARS GUSTAFSSON

Stories
of Happy People

Translated from the Swedish by
Yvonne L. Sandstroem and John Weinstock

Originally published as *Berättelser om lyckliga människor* by P. A. Nordstedt & Söners Förlag, Stockholm, in 1981. This English translation is published by arrangement with Carl Hanser Verlag, Munich.

"A Water Story" was published, in a somewhat different translation, in *The Paris Review*, #93, Fall 1984 (Copyright © 1984 by The Paris Review). An earlier translation of "Greatness Strikes Where It Pleases" appeared in *New Directions in Prose and Poetry 48.*

Manufactured in the United States of America
First published clothbound and as New Directions Paperbook 616 in 1986
Published simultaneously in Canada by Penguin Books Canada Limited

Library of Congress Cataloging-in-Publication Data
Gustafsson, Lars, 1936–
    Stories of happy people.
    (A New Directions Book)
    Translation of: Berättelser om lyckliga människor.
    1. Gustafsson, Lars, 1936–   —Translations,
English.   I. Title.
PT9876.17.U8A27   1986   839.7'374   85-31052
ISBN 0-8112-0977-6
ISBN 0-8112-0978-4 (pbk.)

New Directions Books are published for James Laughlin
by New Directions Publishing Corporation
80 Eighth Avenue, New York 10011

"Fundamentally complex living systems can be defined as systems which can delay the breakdown catastrophe for some time by organizing themselves in a more complex way for as long as possible."

Fritz Cramer

On a certain level of complication, let us say when a needle has been lost in a haystack or a child in a too-large landscape, there is no longer the possibility of *searching*.
We have to *find*, blindly in the darkness.

Contents

Stories
of Happy People

Uncle Sven and the Cultural Revolution

For Max and Marianne

Uncle Sven was a research engineer at the Iron Works and lived in one of the houses up on the hill.

He was the only person in Trummelsberg who knew exactly at which longitude and latitude he lived: in Trummelsberg, the sun rises exactly eight minutes, twenty-nine seconds later than in Stockholm, because of westerly time difference; accordingly, it sets eight minutes, twenty-nine seconds later.

Actually, all of this only applies at the summer solstice, since Trummelsberg is situated at a latitude of 59° 12' N; consequently, it receives a somewhat larger portion of polar darkness in the winter than does the capital, due to the inclination of the earth's axis.

These calculations were caused by the circumstance that while Uncle Sven was pursuing his education, he had found an American wife—as the years went by, she turned into the most enchanting little blue-haired troll who, all her life, stubbornly refused to learn Swedish, so that the salespeople in the Konsum supermarket finally had to learn to speak American in order to understand what she wanted. She always played the violin in church on solemn occasions.

This American wife—her name, by the way, was Frankie—considered that it went without saying there should be roses in a garden, lots of roses: Queen Elizabeth, Pink, Trotter's Glory, and so forth.

Now Trummelsberg has never been a particularly good place for roses. No doubt the winters do something to them that isn't good for them, and what the winters don't do is done by all those peculiar red and black ants that thrive so nicely in the morainal sand of northern Västmanland.

After a number of growing seasons that were exceptionally

1

poor for roses, Uncle Sven maintained that the latitude was quite impossible for them, that there wasn't a single person who had succeeded in growing anything but briar roses in Trummelsberg. Since his wife's answer was that it was absolute nonsense, in the States people grew roses way up in the Finger Lakes district, a slight marital dispute arose during which Sven quickly proved that New York is actually at the latitude of Madrid and Austin, Texas, the latitude where the Bay of Aqaba runs into the Red Sea, and that a confounded northern latitude such as Trummelsberg's is only to be found among the frozen rivers of Labrador. When Frankie stubbornly kept insisting that the placement of Europe in relation to the North Pole couldn't possibly be as bad as all that, Sven decided to tackle the problem in earnest.

Actually, it was quite a simple matter.

The south wall of the house, where the roses drooped from the trellis in the spring light, had an east-west orientation. With the aid of an old army compass and a declination chart, it was quite easy to figure out that the wall faced as due south as could reasonably be expected.

Using his grandfather's excellent cylinder escapement watch and the radio's time signal at one p.m., (the equivalent of noon, Greenwich Mean Time), with an eye on the shrinking shadow of the flagpole, it should be quite easy to determine in how many minutes and seconds following the time signal the shadow was at its shortest.

It turned out not to be that easy. The first day, the sun went behind a cloud right at one o'clock and stayed there for the rest of the afternoon.

The next day, there was brilliant sunshine, but this time the lab director at the Iron Works called to say it had been decided that Sven was going to China with Johansson from Sales to confer with a steel factory outside Shanghai.

Sven liked Johansson. They sometimes played golf together. In China, the Cultural Revolution was in full swing, for this was in the beginning of April 1968.

Uncle Sven had only a vague notion of China, and the words

2

"Cultural Revolution" evoked only vague associations with amateur theatrical groups. His wife seldom passed up any of the amateur theatricals in the community, although she still, after thirty years, couldn't understand Swedish. As a young girl, she had been with an amateur group in Boston.

Anyway, there was nothing to do but to say yes. Big business deals were afoot, and if Sven could bring in his passport after lunch so they could send it special delivery to Stockholm, the two gentlemen might perhaps be able to leave as early as the following Thursday.

"Do you think I should bring my table tennis paddle," Sven said.

Johansson wondered if it would be any use bringing his golf clubs.

When he returned to the trellis, naturally the shadow had grown too long again. The third day it rained. The fourth, Uncle Sven had to go out for lunch. It had to do with the trip to China: what interested the Chinese steel syndicate was the possibility of forging propeller shafts thirty meters long from a special kind of steel.

"The Americans are doing it. The Germans have been doing it since 1905. It's feasible, but you've got to have the right tools," Sven said. "Do they really have that size equipment?"

The fifth day, everything went perfectly. Eight minutes, twenty-nine seconds. Determining latitude was easy when you had the exact meridian. The flagpole was excellent, because it provided the same precision as the giant theodolites of the old Indian princes, with whose aid it had been possible to calculate the latitude of distant stars. True, it became necessary to walk rather far into the neighbors' garden, watch and all. His neighbor, the former cabowner Hansson, was rather surprised when Sven started using his steel measuring tape to measure the distance from the base of the flagpole to a mark right in the middle of the carefully raked approach to Hansson's garage. This led to certain explanations, even to some harsh words, and Sven returned to a belated lunch feeling that Hansson had never really appreciated

3

the difference between sine and hyperbolic sine. Nevertheless, by the time he was ready for coffee he had calculated his private latitude on his pocket calculator: 59 degrees, 12 minutes and 34 seconds North.

This was a substantial piece of information, and Frankie asked if she shouldn't heat up the coffee, which had gone cold.

Roses or no roses: her husband was a marvelous guy.

They didn't reach Shanghai until Sunday. Shanghai was a sea of red flags, posters, pictures of Mao, the streets so packed with short, amicably curious people with little red books in their hands that sometimes their taxi, whose springs had seen better days and which smelled more strongly of gasoline inside than out, got completely stuck in the crowds.

Their hotel, a somewhat nondescript but enormous building with endless corridors, was so large that there was a hall porter's desk on every floor. Sven and Johansson from Sales followed gratefully in the steps of their shy interpreter. The bag with Johansson's golf clubs was heavy and dragged on the hall carpet. He tried to make the dragging as unobtrusive as possible.

He hoped that the Shanghai golf courses would still be open, even though the Cultural Revolution was in progress.

They hardly had time to wash off the dust and dirt of travel before new gentlemen from the steel syndicate arrived to welcome them. One of them was such a distinguished personage that he was dressed in black wool instead of blue. The meeting took place over a cup of tea in the hotel lobby, so the golf clubs were not in evidence.

"Is either of you interested in sports?" asked the black-clad man with amiable courtesy.

Perhaps golf was an expression of the profoundest bourgeois decadence? Following a sudden impulse, Johansson said, "I play table tennis. I actually play quite a bit of table tennis."

"I hope," said the worthy representative of the Tien Ting steel syndicate, "that we shall be fortunate enough, during the weeks ahead of us, to be able to find a player who can offer you

4

something which bears at least some resemblance to a sporting opposition."

A secretary made a quick notation.

In the streets, crowds of people eddied back and forth all night like the sea; the red flags seemed to have a life of their own under the streetlights, fluttering and moving: a large, frightening waterfall of people gravitating to some distant place.

The first conference took place punctually at eight o'clock. Slightly breathless after a taxi ride through an ocean of cyclists who did not seem to be adhering to any kind of human traffic regulations, the gentlemen from Trummelsberg arrived at the steel syndicate and were ushered into a conference room in a plain annex.

This, too, was surprisingly full of people. Everybody had the little red book in his hand. A secretary quickly passed a copy to each of the gentlemen from Trummelsberg who, after an interval of bewildered page-turning, found that the text was in English.

The gentleman in the black suit led them in song. Then followed a reading, during which one of the interpreters obliged Uncle Sven with the right page in the English edition.

In Sven's opinion, the book was essentially sound: it breathed forth profound optimism. When his turn came, he wet his fingers, found a good place, and read, "Say what you think, clearly and without reservation."

He looked around. Everyone seemed to approve.

Johansson found something about Party work on the next page; this turned out a bit strange. But the next time they came around to Uncle Sven, he was prepared and read in a strong, loud voice, his English heavily overlaid with a Västmanland accent. "Study diligently."

After twenty minutes and another song, they sat down at the conference table.

After another twenty minutes of reports, questions, and misunderstandings, Uncle Sven realized that the problem was simple and unsolvable.

If you want to make—that is to say, forge—propeller shafts thirty meters in length from steel billets, you have to have drop forges that can handle a length of thirty meters.

The longest drop forge the steel syndicate possessed could, with some dangerous modifications, manage six meters.

They actually supposed it would be possible to forge five of them, six meters each, and then weld the ends together.

If Uncle Sven had been at home in Trummelsberg, he'd have laughed out loud. Now he leaned across the table instead, rather red in the face, agitatedly leafing back and forth through his little book.

Never, in all his adult life, had he encountered such absolute insanity. To weld together a propeller shaft, an object that would have to tolerate the regular weight of hundreds of kilotons, hour after hour, month after month, at the most crucial spot in a ship, with unavoidable microscopic tensile stress, a very large torque—a shaft that would have to tolerate all this, welded together!

Evidently they had flown him around the world to make fun of him. The lab director was going to hear some straight talking when Sven returned home.

Angrily, he kept turning the pages of his little book.

It certainly was the most peculiar text he'd ever come across.

Only after a while did he become aware that the respectful silence in the room was due to the fact that everyone was waiting for him to speak.

The only thing that surfaced in his mind was the word *Kohlsauerstoffverfahren*.

What on earth was *Kohlsauerstoffverfahren*? He must have heard it on some earlier occasion.

Yes of course, in Fulda in 1931, at Professor Eiseleben's, during a lecture one Thursday morning after a formidable drinking party in a duelling students' fraternity. But what the hell did *Kohlsauerstoffverfahren* mean?

An extremely slow cooling-down process, prolonged day after day, while pulverized coal and oxygen were added, accomplishing the exchange which bonded the complex crystals more securely to each other until no join could be detected, not even with a metallurgical X-ray microscope. But how was it done? His lecture notes from Fulda had been confiscated by Nazi customs agents on his way home at Christmas, 1933.

Had anything as strange as *Kohlsauerstoffverfahren* ever existed? Or was it something he had dreamt? If there ever had been such a process, why hadn't it been used? Why wasn't it *world-renowned*?

And, if it existed—and that was the most provoking thought— why in the world hadn't he thought of it during his twenty-two years in Trummelsberg but here instead, surrounded by a bunch of strange people who slavishly read from a red confirmation book? Why here?

"My dear friends," said Uncle Sven. "I do not wish to make a pronouncement today. The extent and difficulty of the problem force me to a thorough study of the *Quotations from Chairman Mao*."

A sigh of approval went through the room. Evidently, this gentleman from the Trummelsberg Iron Works wasn't as uninformed as one would have imagined, considering his European bald head and always dirty glasses.

In the night he slept fitfully and had strange dreams. Once he was with Grandma Tekla at a revival meeting in the Mission House up on the hill at Halvarsviken; people were singing and bearing witness, and the cast-iron stove in the old Mission House was steaming. Another time, he was in the yard of the high school in Västerås, pursued by a mean physics teacher who insisted that he was the one who had thrown an iceball through the window of the lab right after Morning Prayer.

The old principal, Landtmanson, regarded him with large, clear, reproachful eyes behind his pince-nez. He shook his head. What a wicked young man! "But I really didn't throw any iceball," Uncle Sven complained to the silence of his Chinese hotel room, turning, for the twentieth time, on his Chinese hotel pillow, which was much too hard and full of sharp corners.

Brown-shirted Nazi students were singing and shouting. The

echoes bounced between the old buildings in Fulda, and Sven
didn't want to hear and put his fingers in his ears behind the tall,
dusty windows of the university library. Fritz, the old janitor, in
black tail coat with strange-looking sleeve protectors, moved up
and down the aisles, carrying periodicals with slips of paper
inserted into them.

If he could only remember the name of that damn periodical.
Or who had written the article.

He woke again, in a cold sweat, and pulled the curtain to one
side. Empty, abandoned in the dim light of dawn, the all too wide
Chinese street stretched toward still whiter, still more monotonous districts. Incomprehensible characters on red cotton streamers fluttered from tall poles in the faint morning breeze. Two
cyclists in blue broadcloth were on their way down the street with
some kind of lunchboxes in their bike baskets. They weren't
speaking to each other; they just kept pedaling energetically.

Well, it could look like that at home at the Works, too. "You
have to be satisfied so long as things are going all right," his Papa
used to say. And here he, Sven, lay, sweating and feeling as if he
might be coming down with gastritis, with obvious rheumatism in
his left shoulder, pondering how the People's Republic might
increase the size of their merchant marine.

As an old member of the Mission congregation and resident of
Bergslagen, he was used to trying to do what he could. He fell
asleep at the first true light of dawn. And life suddenly seemed
quite meaningless to him.

"Constructing apparatus for drop-forging that will be able to
handle thirty-meter pieces will take at least twelve months. It's
possible that it might be done a bit faster in the U. S., where they
have experience with very large pieces in the engineering industry,
but naturally you have to consider costs at this juncture."

Mr. Wong, a white-haired, clean-shaven, very pleasant man,
listened attentively. He, too, was wearing the Mao button in his
lapel. He had wise, somewhat tired, but smiling eyes.

"Sooner or later it will have to be done, of course. The Chinese

8

ship-building industry has to learn to handle really large pieces. The cost must be weighed against what will be gained in experience. In all probability, you will run into some disappointments along the way. At any rate, the obstacle is fatal as far as a normal construction timetable is concerned. Trummelberg's Iron Works would probably be able to deliver the propeller shafts in a somewhat shorter time, but the order would necessitate an adjustment there as well. On the other hand, they have been manufacturing propeller shafts in Trummelsberg as far back as World War I. Isn't it a fact that the German submarine fleet in World War I was driven by propellers marked with the famous H, the quality symbol that signified the Counts Hermanssons' quality industry?"

Mr. Wong remained politely silent.

He, Uncle Sven, realized of course that for his company it would mean a large order if their Chinese friends really wanted to entrust them with it. But estimates would take some time. One would have to make a rather extensive total projection. He was prepared to try to get the preliminary calculations started by telegram, but it would take at least a few weeks.

Mr Wong nodded in consideration.

On the other hand it was written, "Say what you think, clearly and without reservation." And if he, Uncle Sven, was really going to say what he thought, clearly and without reservation, it might surprise his Chinese friends.

"How so?" asked Mr. Wong, and the young interpreter, happy to have something to do at last, obediently translated, "How so?"

The atmosphere was a bit strained. Uncle Sven made an unnecessary noise with the china lid of his teacup, only to find that the cup was empty. With a gesture which betrayed a certain, very slight, but still discernible impatience, Mr. Wong sent one of the secretaries to fill it in the anteroom.

"Well," said Uncle Sven, "it's easy to tell yourself that the world is old, that everything has already been done. And in one way Chairman Mao is quite right: perhaps the world is very young. Perhaps there are thousands of untried possibilities just around the corner. Perhaps it's only we who are tired, who have become used to giving up, calling resignation by the name of truth, calling everything that represents an obstacle reality and every hope, unreality.

"I can quite well imagine that the Chairman is right, that it's actually—without any use of violence of course," he added with a cautious sidelong glance through his horn-rimmed glasses, "—the right thing to do to make a revolution.

"But on the other hand, Chairman Mao is quite wrong. Everything has been done before. History is always the strongest. Whatever you think, there is always some old Chinese or Greek philosopher who has thought it before. Confucius, for instance, a truly admirable Chinese philosopher."

Silence prevailed in the room as the interpreter continued to intone his translation—he had a bit of trouble with Confucius, but quickly realized that the gentleman had meant K'ung Fu-tse. The silence fell a few degrees, but Uncle Sven continued polishing his glasses with a dazzling white handkerchief from the left-hand pocket of his wool suit.

"As a boy, you find the world ridiculous; you want to do something entirely different. As an old man, you discover that you have done the usual things. You were only a letter in a text that was discovered long ago. Just as the rarest characters reappear again and again in a text if only it's long enough, you always, sooner or later, find that you are the repetition of something that existed already." Wasn't it a fact that he himself, as a boy, had been expelled from school, so that he had to complete his studies in Germany, where darkness was falling with greater and greater swiftness? Shouldn't he know what rebellion meant, he who had once said "Shut up, you old fart" to Landtmansson, principal of the Västerås highschool—a murmur went through the assembly when the interpreters at last collected themselves sufficiently to render a translation of this enormity. Well, he could understand what the Chairman meant in his excellent little red book. It was correct and, at the same time, it was wrong.

Now to get right down to it, there was, if his memory served him right, in *Archiv für Metallurgie*, volume XXXII, 1927, an article in which the so-called Eisenfels Process was described, that is to say Professor Mauritz Eisenfels' so-called *Kohlsauerstoff-Verfahren*, a method for the production of extremely strong crystal bonding through post-treatment of forged steel through the continuous, slow addition of oxygen and deoxidized coal. As far as he, Uncle Sven, knew, this method had never been tried on a large scale, but there was absolutely nothing to stop you from trying. Like thousands of other ideas, this one had lain dormant after the professor disappeared into some concentration camp, in night and fog, behind barbed wire. In short, during a night of study of Comrade Chairman Mao's writings, he had become convinced that his friends were on the right track. It had to be possible to assemble a propeller shaft from separate forged-steel segments. If they were successful, they would be the first in the world to have accomplished this feat. He himself felt rather tired after a very restless night and now wished to retire to his hotel, but if he were needed for consultation, he would of course be at their disposal on the following day.

Respectfully, they accompanied him all the way to his waiting car. One secretary carried his briefcase, another his umbrella. In the conference room, secretaries and interpreters struggled frantically, comparing their notes.

The discussions in the Planning Committee of the steel syndicate assumed the proportions of a waterfall. Every telephone line was fraught to the breaking point.

Johansson from Sales had the opportunity, a bit later the same week, to play table tennis. The hall was quite large and "a few young people" had been found who at least should be able to offer "a somewhat sporting opposition."

Johansson lost the first game 21–2. He succeeded in making his opponent, an extremely polite and quiet young man, a bit nervous with his first two serves, since the opponent had never seen anything like it. After that he lost 21–0, 21–0.

He never was quite sure whether he had played one of the club's lesser talents or a candidate for the world championship, but as time went by, he tended to describe it as a match against a world champion.

The Works made Uncle Sven retire two years later. Those last two years, he was considered too old and tired for the demands of foreign travel. When he retired, he bought an excellent Japanese telescope. You might see him occasionally on winter evenings, in a fur jacket from his army days, with his fur cap pulled down over his ears, trying to aim his Barlow lense at the Black Cloud in Pegasus, at Andromeda's shining, mysterious disc, and at the evasive moons of Jupiter, where perhaps is germinating the only life in the solar system that would diminish our own solitude.

On the wall of his living room Uncle Sven has a reminder of his trip, an exquisite painting from the Ming period. It is called "On the Way to a Friend with a Lute," and it shows an old man being rowed by a boy across a mountain lake at sunset, to a small hut on a forested island. The lights in the hut have just been lit. The friend is standing on the dock waiting. The shadows of the mountains deepen.

Frankie, who occasionally dusts the picture, a gift from some steel syndicate in Shanghai, regards it with dreaming and uncertain eyes.

Just *how* tremendously valuable this gift is she has never comprehended.

The Four Railroads of Iserlohn

1

Iserlohn, a small, surprisingly friendly town in a mountainous region close to the French border, had during the unusually severe and, above all, terribly snowy winter of 1979, at least four different railroads.

The four railroads had only an occasional and, so to speak, purely spiritual contact with one another. It's hard to say which one was the most important; that would depend on what perspective they were viewed from and, in particular, from *whose.*

And perhaps it isn't so important that everything should be important.

Of these four railroads, there actually was only one that ever left the town.

There is an explanation, which we will soon get to.

However, the story begins long before we come to the snowy winter of 1979, actually so snowy that during a couple of weeks in January, it was quite possible to ski all the way in from the snow-clad heights outside town and in the Mendener Strasse. The newspapers were full of indignant letters to the editor in which people complained about the huge amount of snow, about the poor snow removal and bad sanding of the streets.

With reason, several of the letter writers asked what in God's name would happen if a true catastrophe were to occur in Iserlohn, when a few days of ordinary snowfall evidently could create such chaos.

But in October of 1978, nobody could have guessed that the winter would be so severe.

It was a great, golden, friendly season. The apples ripened and the autumn woods slowly assumed the golden color so characteristic of the oak and beech stands of the region, when the great fall at last appears with rich light and shorter days.

The air was still quite warm when I arrived in Iserlohn on one of the many journeys that I made at the end of the '70s.

No one met me at the station. I lugged my beastly heavy suitcase, my almost worn-out portable, and my tennis bag up to the only hotel in town that was somewhat decent, Zum Alten Post. Before I reached the shade of the hotel lobby, the sweat was pouring off me profusely.

I cursed the organizers of my visit, who hadn't had the sense to meet me at the station and who hadn't reserved a room for me, either.

My name was not on the register. Fortunately, though, there were rooms. Soon I was standing in the shower.

I had been traveling quite a bit the last few weeks. Hotel rooms had been my bedrooms, but my daily workroom was a train compartment, now on one stretch, now on another. I had been to Basel and Zurich; I had spent a few warm and contemplative days in Vienna, sitting with my spiral notebooks in various cafés; familiar Berlin could be glimpsed on the horizon—yes, it was an extensive, labyrinthine journey, because I was traveling around reading publicly from a novel that had just been published in German.

After my shower and a change into fairly respectable and light clothing, I went out into the town of Iserlohn and looked around. I left the central business district—which, truth to tell, was not particularly impressive—behind me, climbed up steep streets with deciduous trees blushing in autumn colors, successively becoming more and more beautiful, and making friendly arches across quiet, stone-paved roadways.

I strolled along pensively, pondering problems that were entirely my own, when it suddenly struck me that perhaps I ought to get back to the hotel and find the hosts for that evening's reading.

It was already about six—the time at which I would usually be having dinner with some local cultural potentate, discussing literary life in Europe. It really *was* peculiar that I hadn't heard from anybody.

About this time, I realized that I must have lost my way. Evidently, I'd forgotten where I was walking: I mean, I had forgotten to memorize the streetcorners.

Just as I started to give up hope—all the streets seemed to return to the same place, a kind of square or plaza with a peaceful fountain, large, green trees, and patrician villas with green shutters—I realized that I ought to go into one of the houses.

The largest villa looked as if it contained some kind of office. Only when I had let the heavy oak door fall shut behind me did I realize that I was standing in a conservatory.

A long corridor with doors and a particular piece of music behind each door.

From behind one door there issued the beautiful, hesitant introduction to Bach's Trio Sonata; from behind another, the sound of a viola playing its part, a bit isolated and abstract, from one of Brahm's string quartets; and from behind a third door, the second of Bach's cello suites.

I chose the cello suite. Bach has always been closest to my heart.

It was a young woman bending over the cello, somewhat ponderous, somewhat melancholy, with an almost maternal relation to the instrument. I've always found something sexually exciting about women playing the cello; their way of stabilizing the instrument with their left thigh has always intrigued me.

But this young woman—who, by the way, looked pretty good with her long brown hair—treated her cello more as if it were a son.

She stopped in the middle of a precipitous passage from the allemande and looked at me long and carefully. You might almost have thought she had been expecting me. She didn't seem the least bit surprised that I'd looked in but, on the other hand, a bit surprised that I looked the way I did.

"You don't look at all like your photographs," she said.

"Most of my photographs here in Germany are quite old," I said.

"But couldn't you have sent some more recent ones," she said.

"I'm quite satisfied with my looks as they are," I said. "I've

15

never been handsome, but neither have I ever claimed to be. Some of my friends think that I've got an 'agreeable' face. I suppose that means they've gotten used to it."

"O.K.," she said, as if she'd come to a decision. "We'll go downtown and have some beer. We can always talk to each other for a bit. You don't have a car, I take it?"

Resolutely, she put the cello away and closed the book of Bach's cello suites. When she stood up, she suddenly looked a little older. But it was still difficult to tell whether she was thirty or thirty-five.

She had fine, what I'm accustomed to calling "humorous," lines around her eyes. She put on a simple but well-tailored coat, made a sign that meant something along the lines of , "Just a moment, I have to take care of something unpleasant," and disappeared into a room where she quarreled furiously and openly with somebody who might have been her boss. What do I know?

"O.K.," she said once more when she reappeared, this time with something cool in her voice. "Now I'm ready. We can leave now. We can go to a nice bar I know."

By this time, I was so fascinated that I had completely forgotten my evening reading. Or it could have been that I'd already managed to tell myself that this strong, vital young woman would be able to solve the whole problem of finding those damn organizers and also the bookstore, college, or library where I was supposed to turn up and read from my book. Dusk fell, the streetlights were lit, and her little VW hummed resolutely down the hills of Iserlohn.

Everything was very cozy.

There was nothing special about this bar, apart from the fact that it sported the most beautiful beer tap I'd ever seen. I could imagine traveling to Iserlohn just to see this tap. It had stature: it shone cold and brilliant, made of a blue faience which made you think of the high point of Eastern Islamic art, the wonderful, coldly blue mosques on the way to Bengal. Isfahan would have been proud of such a beer tap.

I asked if I could get her something.

"Please, a small glass of light."

The bartender was very slow, very careful to remove the foam. I had a feeling—but of course I might have been mistaken—that he watched us the whole time.

Meanwhile, an older man entered, dressed in a worn raincoat and a typically British sports cap. He looked around and then sat down with us.

"I'm very sorry if I'm disturbing you," he said, "but there's really no room at any other table. I'm very careful not to disturb other people in public places, least of all couples in love."

"Oh, you're not disturbing us at all," I said, quickly in order to prevent any misunderstanding.

The young woman did not seem to be in total agreement.

"Did you come by train?" the older man asked.

"Yes, by the three o'clock train," I said.

"Then your life was in my hands," he said. "I'm a minor railway employee. I'm at the signal box. We have responsibility for the central traffic control all the way to Gütersloh."

"Oh, all the way to Gütersloh," I said. "Good God! Would you please repeat what you just said?"

"We have the responsibility for the central traffic . . . "

"Just the last word," I said. "What was that name?"

"Gütersloh," the older man said helpfully.

"I'll be damned," I said, carefully pulling my much-folded and scribbled-on reading program from my pocket.

"Yes, I'm a minor railway employee," said the man, with great seriousness and with sudden dignity. "And I do my job, actually I do it with the same blind precision as an electronic machine. I may have the worst hangover some mornings, but the signal box gives you no scope for imagination, no improvisation, you know. There are times in the day when I have an express train in either direction every three minutes. Then you've got no time for a spiritual life."

"It's strange," I said, to myself mostly, putting the confounded reading program back in my pocket, "but I seem to have believed all along that *Iserlohn* and *Gütersloh* are exactly the same. But of course that isn't so. They're different towns."

"Gütersloh is an unpleasant, somewhat vulgar and upstart kind of place compared to Iserlohn. No one who had the choice would possibly prefer Gütersloh to Iserlohn," the young woman said, very decidedly.

"I was supposed to give a reading there tonight," I told her.

"I make my living as a railroad man, but actually I am something else," said the older man. "I am a disciple of Kierkegaard. Sometime in the next century, they'll be having lecture series about me at every American university."

"What is it you write?" I asked.

"Moral philosophy. I'm writing a great work of moral philosophy. It will encompass all the contradictions of our times, just as Kierkegaard was able to encompass all the contradictions of his times in his work."

"How do you find the time?" I asked respectfully, because life's experience has taught me that when someone describes himself as a great, very important genius, he is, quite contrary to what the common herd suppose, generally correct. "How do you find the time? Are there any people here in Iserlohn you can talk to about such problems," I said, something which may have been guileless on my part.

The signal box man's eyes darkened. Menacingly and gloomily, he looked into his own open hands, as if the answer were to be read there.

"I write on Sunday mornings, from early on until my wife has fixed lunch."

"Does she get to read your manuscript?" I said. (Once you've gotten onto the wrong track in a conversation, it's almost impossible to get away from it.)

"She doesn't have the slightest idea what I'm doing, and not the least bit of understanding either. I'm absolutely alone in what I'm doing. Once upon a time I had friends. I've betrayed them."

"How?"

"I have sacrificed them to social advancement."

"How?"

"When I was still young, an ordinary railway man, I had lots of communist friends. Simple young workers, but with intellectual interests."

18

"And as a signal box foreman you consider that you're too good to associate with your former comrades?"

"Too good—not at all. Only that a signal box man with communist friends is a complete impossibility. For an enemy of the constitution to sit watching an express train in either direction every three minutes—it's quite impossible, any idiot can see that. There's a dividing line. Then you have to choose. Signal box or communism—both are excellent, but not both at once. You have to choose. That's where moral choice begins."

"What you're saying is much too elegant, much too philosophical for me," I said. "It's above my head. If I didn't know that you're a great philosophical genius perhaps I'd dare debate you—but as things are—on no condition. Let's visit that fantastic beer tap again. It entices me; like an Abbasidic mosque in an East Turkoman desert," I added.

When I got back from the bar, laboriously balancing three foaming schooners of the iron-rich, tasty local beer, the brilliant man had gone, whether temporarily or for good was difficult to say.

"That must be fun," said the young woman. "You know, I've always wanted a model railroad. I've always been so fascinated by the *network* itself in what's called the *railroad network*, the possible combinations, the secret life that a big railroad always lives; just imagine, there's always some train on its way somewhere, day and night, always some train in motion.

"But since I never managed to own a model railway as a child—and"—she gave me a nervous side-glance which I didn't quite understand—"since I don't have much hope of acquiring one now, I've always had to be content with the ordinary railroad.

"That is to say, I write angry letters to the director of the Bundesbahn every time an express train doesn't arrive on time. And I usually write quite furiously every time they don't hold connecting trains when an express train is late. That's an abominable abuse of power. I simply cannot abide it."

She hit the marble table top with her, truthfully, very small hand, her exquisite musician's hand—but not with such force that there was the smallest risk that she'd injure it—and leaned toward me. She took, truth to tell, both my hands in hers, looked me deep in the eye with a pair of large eyes at once warm, honest, and despairing, and said: "Will we ever understand each other, the two of us? Will we ever be able to live together?"

The last question seemed to me a bit quick and intimate to be addressed to someone who had looked in for a moment to ask directions, and perhaps I would have said so, but at that very moment, the railroad employee returned.

He had also got beer, but of a quite different, much darker kind. He sat down with a sigh.

"No. My wife understands nothing. My fellow workers have no idea of it. My time is not sufficient for it. I've never met another person who writes. And if you only knew how little it amounts to on a Sunday morning. Only a few bits of paper in the bottom of a cigar box. I collect them in the bottoms of cigar boxes, you see, cigar boxes that I've arranged according to a special classification system. But it amounts to little, very little, on a Sunday morning. Good God, what wouldn't I be able to do if I had every day to myself and didn't have to watch these confounded express trains with their fat, bloated, unintelligent passengers. Why do they want to travel?"

"You know," the young woman said, "if I had your job I'd look at it quite differently. I'd consider myself as having access to a large, wonderful model railroad. On a scale of one to one."

"Except that a model on a scale of one to one can never be surveyable. It ends up over the horizon, *you can't follow the trains all the time.*"

"Perhaps the fact is," said the young woman, "that literature is a whole lot easier to deal with than life. Literature is a small-scale model."

And in life the trains disappear over the horizon.

We kept talking in this vein for a good long time. And I have to admit that I had quite a bit to drink, for the young woman was making me nervous. She seemed to want much too much all at once.

The railroad man finally mounted his bicycle, somewhat unsteadily. He said that he was on duty sometime the following afternoon and evidently counted on being sober by then.

His goodbyes were somewhat long-winded—well, such things happen when someone's had a bit too much. All the time, I had the woman in the back of my mind, so to speak—I had figured out exactly what to say to her. I certainly hadn't forgotten her.

When I turned around, she had disappeared without a trace. Believe me—without a trace!

I left the pub, looked around. Nothing but empty, sleeping streets, the mild, warm autumn wind rustling in yellow leaves around me: not a person as far as the eye could see. No, not in the Ladies, either.

2

During the ensuing winter, a horrendous amount of snow fell. In Chicago, there was a period in January when almost all normal activity ceased; in London, people stopped going to work when snowfall and strikes put an end to almost all normal life. We have to be clear that we are living on the downhill slope, historically speaking—from the summit of industrialism, which must have occurred some time early in the '50s, the world slopes downward, and I don't think much can be done about it.

In Iserlohn, there were no such catastrophic conditions. A few old ladies broke their hips. The papers published some letters to the editor concerning the poor snow removal; a few bold skiers tried to see whether you could get from the town mountain all the way to Mendener Strasse.

Let's suppose that after some time the young woman put an ad in the paper, a new ad, in a new paper (if one of my theories is correct), and found an incredibly handsome and virile Frenchman, who furthermore was such a good flutist that he could talk to her about Bach for whole afternoons at a stretch.

With her cello and her other belongings in four big boxes, she moved out of the apartment collective where she had been living for a long time into a huge, old-fashioned apartment. With her new husband, she moved into a quiet house in which three families were living above one another on different floors.

Still unused to the sounds in the new building, she would lie there listening to the darkness when, as she regularly did, she woke at three or four in the morning. It might be a freezer starting up with a surprising click and a whirring noise. Or it might be the sound of a distant express train making its way through the first heavy snowfall of the morning.

In the glow from the streetlight outside the window, she could see the snowflakes, small and mobile the way they always are when the temperature is considerably below freezing, dancing around in whirls.

She worried that perhaps she didn't get enough sleep—a cellist needs a lot of sleep—and that her restless movements might wake her husband. And she calmed down again by thinking soothing thoughts. Of long journeys to warmer, less snowy places. Of the trains which manfully, without fear, moved far into the thickening snow.

Of people's dreams, which perhaps met in secret and crossed inside the thickening snowfall of deep sleep.

Sometimes, it was one of the cats in the building that, in one lightening-quick bound, disappeared through a cleverly constructed cellar opening on the ground floor.

She realized that she ought to go down, on some pretext, and have coffee with the owner of the house, an old lady who apparently had no husband but a son instead, a perpetual "student" at the University of Aachen, who nevertheless always seemed to stay at home with his mother.

He seemed to be already in his thirties.

January trudged slowly on.

Between her cello lessons, her orchestra rehearsals (they were going to perform Tchaikovsky's Sixth by the end of February), and her new married life, she hardly had time to arrange her books in the new apartment.

One Sunday morning, as she was standing on the landing with

an empty wooden box that had to be carried down into the cellar, the gentleman who lived in the apartment above walked past with a huge package under his arm.

They greeted each other politely. During at least the first few weeks when she lived in the house, there had also been a wife to say hello to, a small, slight, slim, blonde woman.

She hadn't been in evidence lately.

"Guess what I've got in this box," the gentleman said playfully. He looked unusually happy. His small, brown mustache waved with unaccustomed hopefulness in the breeze; there was a glimpse of a patch of unclouded sky in his eyes. It was evident that something had happened to him.

"You've got a model railroad in your box," she said, entering the guessing game right away.

"How on earth did you know that?"

"I don't know. It just occurred to me that that must be it."

"That's fantastic."

"Isn't it?"

"You see: I've gotten divorced. Or more precisely, my wife has abandoned me."

"How sad."

"Yes, in a way. But not in another. She was always so terribly jealous of my model railroad."

"And now, at last, you've got the chance to expand it?"

"No. I'm not expanding it, I'm building a whole new one, on a much smaller scale. That way I'll have room for more tracks. It'll be a lot more *surveyable*."

"You were involved in railroads as a boy."

"Tremendously."

"And now you're returning to the model railroad?"

"You speak as if it were a fault."

"Oh, I didn't mean that at all. It just occurred to me that there's so much privatism these days. We've gotten so far away from 1968, when the collective was everything. I myself have lived in different apartment collectives for the past twelve years. And now I've moved into a three-room apartment with a husband. And

23

when you couldn't stand your wife any longer, you retreated to the paradise of your boyhood, to a surveyable world, the model railroad."

"You speak so frankly and so kindly that I want to answer you frankly. So: what made it so difficult to live with my wife was not that she couldn't tolerate my model railroad."

"Oh, you mean that it was just a symbol for something else?"

"For my world, of the things in the world that were mine and not hers. Or better: for those things in the world that she couldn't wrest from me. My unhappy marriage, a failure from beginning to end, has given me the idea that, at bottom, love is nothing but a form of envy. The attempt to become someone else when you can no longer stand who you are. But, of course, it isn't possible to become someone else."

"And so you've bought a model railroad?"

"And some important parts to complete my old one, which I've brought down from the attic. It was up there in the attic all the time, packed in boxes."

The young woman was silent for a moment. She thought, "What is it, actually, that we sacrifice for companionship?"

3

What is it that we lose? Perhaps it's something much more valuable than we think.

At night, after her husband had fallen asleep, she remained awake in bed for a long time, dreaming about a model railroad of her own. That was the third railroad of Iserlohn.

She decided that it should be very large, very labyrinthine. It should have tunnels and deep cuts through wild mountains made from papier-mâché, and there should be a harbor with piers, a hint of the sea, where all the tracks would stop, a possibility of death, perhaps, but also of freedom and of change.

And here and there the railroad would come very close to little villages, villages with rather primitive, but not very poverty-stricken appearances, something similar to the villages in northern China, industrious villages, where modern times did not have such a great chance to make themselves felt.

She lay awake in the darkness contemplating the not totally unimportant question of whether the villages should have Christian churches, mosques, or perhaps Buddhist temples, when the annoying thermostat in the freezer kicked in again. Her husband turned in his sleep; he had a very fine, perhaps somewhat pale face.

He was a fine, sensitive human being. Close to others.

How was the railroad to be controlled?

Of course, there had to be a control panel, with buttons and contact breakers to all the points, to all the railroad crossings (with real warning bells), and to all the canal locks and drawbridges.

Or perhaps it would be better to have a small computer controlling the whole thing? She ought to get manuals and instruction booklets, software and hardware, to see what might be done.

But shouldn't chance also be built into a computer like that? A railroad totally without risk, totally without surprises and dangers, totally without challenges and encounters, so to speak, wouldn't it become monotonous in the long run?

She shuddered slightly at the thought.

The annoying freezer started whirring again. She pulled the soft plaid blanket higher up over her shoulders and tried to go back to sleep.

It wasn't easy.

She thought about her neighbor with the railroad.

She thought about student demonstrations in Berlin and Heidelberg—she often had a nightmare that she was running, with hundreds of other people, from police armed with nightsticks. And everyone was fleeing and would flee forever.

Perhaps the policemen, too, were fleeing from something?

Wasn't it true that all the power in the world was based on the same big lie: that the meaning of our lives is located *outside* of ourselves?

But if the meaning couldn't be located anywhere else but *within* us, in the darkness that is your own self, beyond all moral traps, then we also have to remain forever unknown to ourselves. Was that how it was?

Then her husband started to snore, very light, very refined little snores.

She became aware of a faint feeling of happiness mounting, a happiness of some new, unknown kind.

Like the happiness before a long journey.

4

It was, as I have already mentioned, a terrible winter. It didn't let up until the beginning of April.

One Friday afternoon, right at sunset, she looked in on the lady on the first floor to pay her month's rent.

All winter she had been meaning to invite the two of them, the mother with her stiff but not completely unfriendly face and the son, to have coffee and cookies. It is necessary to have a reasonably friendly relationship with your landlady.

They were just having dinner. The mother was ponderous, like a primordial mother, one who forgives us nothing but who, on the other hand, doesn't deny us anything either.

Her son pale, eating earnestly, always with a touch of a cold. That was probably his excuse for never managing to get off to the university.

When she entered the room, a silence ensued which might have become oppressive. The room was severely, joylessly furnished. A heavy oak table—or perhaps only stained imitation oak—a picture of the dead father (in uniform, who knows what one) on the sideboard, which was also made from the heavy, black wood that might be oak, with a little mirror inset on top, edged with some silly interlacing of carved wood.

Mother and son now started talking and, as always happens in such cases, they interrupted each other frenetically.

The young woman didn't listen. Instead, she stared in fascination at what was standing on top of the sideboard:

Absolutely perfect in its smallness, completely electrified, a tiny model railroad network.

"But there's the train!"

The son jumped up, his cheeks still full of food, and started a magnificent demonstration. As always when such things are to be shown, not quite everything worked. In one place, there were crossing gates that didn't want to behave very well.

And yet *everything* was completely electrified.

The neighbor on the top floor freed himself more and more, the son remained a son, and the young woman? She pondered.

A building, full of railroads unconnected to each other.

Longing to get away and be home at the same time. The big, manly express locomotives bravely struggling through snowstorms and rain, under mountains and across deep ravines.

"We've got the railroad in our house," said the young woman.

Here ends our impossible story.

The Art of Surviving November

It originated with his wife, who often rendered him harmless by treating him ironically.

She was blonde, pale, determined, coolly possessed by something else.

A prominent amateur equestrian: her black, velvet-covered riding hats, nice to stroke with your fingertips, lay on a high shelf in the hall.

In the bedroom closet, those curiously shaped riding breeches which radiated a sweetish smell of sawdust and horse.

Actually, he was someone who deserved to be treated quite without irony.

He occupied a large, light room on the ground floor with his analyses—for the Industrial Association, for the Economic Institute, not infrequently for UNESCO. He was in great demand.

A sturdy Tandberg tape player played endless Bach partitas in the room while he bent over his pads of graph paper and tables.

In the afternoon, his secretary, Mrs. Sjögren, white-haired, competent, pleasant, came and typed up his morning's work.

The house was large: he had inherited it from a family that had worked in the import business since the mid-nineteenth century. His grandmother had had the first real bathroom in Västerås.

It was situated on a long ridge with a view of half the city. Two enormous glassed-in porches, no less, very hard to heat in the winter.

One was always kept cold, and apples were stored there in cartons, which gave it an unpleasant smell.

And if you opened the door, in the winter, or forgot to close it, hundreds of flies woke up. They misinterpreted the heat and drowned everything out with their horrible buzzing.

And that was unendurable.

There were many memories connected with those porches. The eccentric uncles playing cards in the '30s, spring evenings when the kerosene lamp never had to be lit and you sat there listening to Stravinsky's *The Rite of Spring* with some beautiful blonde girl from the Communal Girls' School up on Mariaberget.

All such girls seemed to have disappeared, turned into diplomats' wives or sopranos.

He could remember the slapping of the uncles' cards, the fizzing of the Vichy water bottles. But he did not remember the tranquil conversations with those girls in the long, pleated skirts of the '50s.

Perhaps, after all, they had pimples on their backs?

In all its grotesque, huge woodenness, with its cowls and weathercocks and wicker furniture and with the modern improvements that he had made over the years, the house was easily worth over a million today.

But of course he couldn't sell it, since he needed it to live in.

Besides, he liked living in Västerås.

In Stockholm, you might easily get knifed nowadays just trying to get from the railroad station to the Finance Department. That had happened to one of his friends just recently.

Of course, he had incorporated himself as a consulting business, and this business rented the house from him as an office and then rented a smaller portion of it back to him as living quarters.

In an age when the Internal Revenue decided what everybody's living quarters should cost and, in practice, how everyone should live, such dodges were a necessity.

He belonged to an elite. Still, he had the feeling of continually being demeaned.

"Sweden," some of his friends used to say, "Sweden has become an impossible country for someone who wants to do something or who can do something."

"There may be hidden advantages in this development," he would reply (to his accountant, for instance, and deign to turn down the amplifier somewhat, the amplifier that, for the fourth time since the start of his workday at eight o'clock, was immersed in one of Johann Sebastian Bach's *great* lute suites, the calm, ascetic, pensive one in D-minor). "Now all *material* motives for belonging to the intellectual elite in a society have gone by the board. It isn't even possible to get the use of a car or a house as a perq because you're definitely more competent than other people. In short, there is no reward for ability.

"This will have two consequences. One is that commerce and administration will be taken over by people of no account, non-entities. People like those who, when we were young, had to be content to be employed by the Swedish National Railroad, become directors of youth hostels, or write poetry books, but now those people will head departments and manage the state-subsidized deficit industries. This will liberate the true intellectual elite in Sweden.

"Of course, some of them will decide to live abroad; they will emigrate at an increasing rate as the public sector grows. These people will devote themselves to miserable heart patients in Houston, Texas, they will run the multinational oil companies that are in need of administrators, they will champion the wretched hospital patients in Zug and in Basel. All this is a familiar story; it has already become reality. But the truly interesting thing concerns the people who stay."

"Is that what you think," said the accountant. He was an eminent gourmet and belonged to several fraternal organizations. Besides, he truly admired his friend in the brown house. "What's going to happen to them?"

"For the first time since the seventeenth century, the intellectuals will be a class without an individual profit motive. We'll get a class of wandering monks, of thinkers, of philosophers. Don't you see? We will have an overcapacity for the transcendental world! We're going to *build cathedrals*, just you wait and see!"

He was a little strange those years. The previous fall, he had experienced something which he called "his breakdown."

Now it was the beginning of November, an unusually warm and kindly one as far as that went. He spoke gently to his wife and was in hopes of surviving the month all right.

Two days later, she opened the car door right in front of a truck in that terribly thoughtless way rather typical of women, but not even then did he say anything much, even though the truck took off the whole damn door, to the tune of a repair bill of about three thousand.

"Why don't you look around to the rear before you open the car door," he asked pleasantly.

He was in one of his preoccupied phases and fighting held no charms for him.

So far there was only one cathedral in the city
and the jackdaws of autumn hovered about it
in dreamy, preparatory whirls.

2

Nobody really knows what a human being is.

The torturers of medieval times, knowledgeable, stubborn, thorough, had been unable to solve this riddle. The clinics of the eighteenth century, with their showers, their water baths, traps, and obstacles cunningly placed in the wanderer's path; the nineteenth century, with its straitjackets; Master Freud, with his cleverly devised transformations and rituals—all of them had left some pocket unexplored.

There was a darkness behind man, and this darkness insisted on sending out signals inconsistent with what was expected of him.

Modern states provided him with a birth number, registered him in data banks, organized him into work details or got him all whipped up in mass meetings. The states used him to industrialize Arctic mines citing his Trotskyite deviation, turned him into a shrunken dwarf in tropical starvation areas or into a babbling alcoholic on the subway with its raw, underground dampness and its pressure of massed rock. Physiologists stuck their silver wires into his brain and saw it react to microscopic, deftly applied electrical charges, let orgasms show up on the screen of the oscillograph as electronic storms, not unlike epileptic fits.

And underneath it all, the odd assumption that it was actually possible to know what a human being is.

Incessantly, from every direction, messages flowed in that showed this assumption to be incorrect.

Human beings always refuted man's idiotic belief that he knows his own depths.

It was the fall of 1977 on Jekyll Island, a small, tropical island with excellent conference hotels off the coast of Georgia.

A tremendous tropical thunderstorm moved across the entire horizon in a fine-veined web.

He was standing by the big picture window, watching how every flash of lightning lit up the mile-wide, dazzlingly white beach where, on your ordinary morning run, you might run into strange-looking crabs running sideways.

And right there, in the rain, an old Indian was fishing. He was wearing an old, crumpled straw hat full of hooks; his fishing rod must have been ten yards long, and his wide pants were sharply outlined against the whiteness.

His way of standing there quite still, impassive in the warm swirl of tropical rain, unmoved by the flaming sky above him and the mad sea, foaming white in front of his frayed pants—everything made the watcher in the window feel happy.

It struck him that, strictly speaking, nobody knows what a human being is.

Because nobody has seen a human being from the outside.

He wanted the woman to come to the window and look.

She hadn't yet decided whether she wanted to or not. She was soft, she was tired, she was very hot: she yawned.

She had put her nightgown back on; her long, probably dyed blonde hair was hanging over the beautiful lace collar. She had strong, round shoulders, breasts a bit heavy, as often happens with American women in their thirties.

He liked her a lot. They asked each other very few questions. He had found her in a bar in Jacksonville—she said that she had just been widowed.

He didn't waste much thought on that. In any case, he had to participate in a seminar on Jekyll Island, and it was September 1977.

Nobody knows what a human being is.

The air conditioning, which was first rate, made him feel chilly.

He crept back into bed with the woman.

The thunderstorm was undoubtedly on the wane. Carefully, very slowly, he nuzzled his face deeper into her armpit, which exuded a mild, damp warmth and a faint smell of Nivea cream.

(He remembered that years ago a girl in Greece had told him the reason for the elongated, practical shape of the necks and caps of Nivea bottles. He remembered it had shocked him.

(Probably he was more easily shocked in those days.)

She came from Houston. She was actually a *very* attractive woman. As is often the case with American women of our generation, it took her a long time to reach orgasm, but when she did, it rolled like long, dull waves, breakers across a distant shore so far removed that few travelers had actually taken the time to visit it.

It struck him that she was *geographically indeterminate* in a manner that, in Europe, only women from West Germany could achieve.

She was a woman without a regional accent, without a hometown; there were no paths, no mountain ridges that she knew better than other people. She was the product of a world with interchangeable settings, one motel just like the other, the reception desk of one elegant agency office just like the other.

How many such desks had she sat behind since finishing college?

He liked women like her. When, through all the impersonal stuff, through the smell of Nivea which substituted for an accent, through the knowledge of how to act, a cool part to play, all this knowledge that for people of an earlier time was knowledge of a landscape, of its labyrinths and possibilities; when, through all this, you found your way to the darkness in them—the darkness which is the only personal thing in a human being—you could become surprised by the great warmth, the wisdom of feeling, the

33

intuition of profound sensual pleasure these women could develop.

"What are you thinking of?" she asked, much later the same night.

"Of the fact that fifty acres of woods are cut down on earth every minute. Did you know that?"

"No. But new trees will grow, won't they?"

"Come sit with me here in the window, and I'll tell you a story. But put something on: the air conditioning is quite cold. Or should we open the window and let some warm air in? There won't be any mosquitoes now, after the storm."

"O.K."

The seminar was quite interesting. Tomorrow would be the start of the third day. It was a company with branch offices in some fifty countries, wanting to develop some kind of common reference system, a common terminology to describe economic development in these respective countries.

Whoever controlled the language also controlled development to a certain extent, since he would control how the problem was to be formulated.

And under any circumstance, it was better to have something like this assigned to the relative objectivity of a multinational concern than to have it controlled by local Mafias, by corrupt political parties, power-mad messiahs, local ministers of domestic affairs bent on taking control of the state with the aid of the secret police. The nut to crack was that, evidently, more than one system of description was needed. They needed one for the hopeful and another one, more difficult to formulate, for the realists.

Servants, equipped with small, electric cars, would be coming to the separate picture-window bungalows which comprised the different parts of the hotel; they would change the sheets and towels and clean up the small, elegant housekeeping kitchens.

Then, just like on all the previous days, the woman would sit, not by the water, not by the seashore (which she considered too wild and windy) but by the swimming pool under the mighty pecans, pregnant with Spanish moss. She would sit in a chair by the warm swimming pool, where children splashed with their families, sit there all afternoon, peacefully immersed in some sci-fi novel.

She really belonged to a different shore, a newer culture, and he welcomed this.

She yawned loudly and reached for his glass, in which there was some bourbon heavily diluted with water (he did not approve of the American habit of mixing alcohol and sex: the alcohol, all too easily, could have a dampening, desensitizing effect, and said,

"Hadn't we better get some sleep? There's another day tomorrow."

"O.K."

He kissed her with real tenderness. With the same tenderness you show for an ancient archeological find. Only with her, it was the exact opposite.

The next day, the same heavy freighters would be out in the sound; one of the TV channels would tell you about the winds all over the Carribean with monotonous obstinacy, minutely detailing everything that might be the beginnings of a hurricane.

She would walk along the shore for a while anyway, at low tide, looking for the tiny breathing holes of the mollusk called *Cornea purpurea*, which had such an exquisite, rose-colored inside.

It was possible to clean out the shells by boiling them in a pan of water in the kitchen.

She thought it was disgusting and had turned the job over to him; there were already a few shells on the kitchen counter.

Their purple-colored insides looked like a secret too carelessly relinquished.

3

Together with the quiet Professor Jantz from Munich, they strolled along the white beach, dressed only in bathing suits.

They had swum a mile or so, but then she'd got frightened by some huge dorsal fins several hundred yards out to sea.

According to the professor, they were not sharks but dolphins.

All three sat down on a silver-colored, sea-polished log and watched the sun slowly enter an immense cloud bank in the northwest, possibly a storm center forming out in the Carribean.

"The year 1866," said the professor, a slightly eccentric specialist in public affairs, a visiting professor at Harvard that fall, "1866 is a hard, dark year in the history of Bavaria. Through the unsuccessful war with Prussia, Bavaria definitely loses her hegemony among the German-speaking peoples.

"King Ludwig II, absolutely bereft of all his illusions about ever being able to play a real historic role, bereft of his friendship with Richard Wagner, who has been driven from Munich after the scandalous affair with Cosima, the wife of the conductor von Bülow, totally bereft of belief in anything even remotely resembling a normal life since his betrothal has been broken off, King Ludwig II of Bavaria leaves his capital and settles, first at the alpine pleasure palace Lindenhof, and several years later at Neuschwanstein, furnished with even greater and more lavish splendor.

"These castles are remarkable, you see, because they are not buildings in the usual sense. They are *representations* of buildings, three-dimensional fantasies about a life that has never been lived anywhere."

"A sort of Disneyland?"

"Yes. But in real earnest. There is not a normal lavatory, not a closet, not even a proper working stove in either of the castles.

"The King's bedroom is a show bedroom, in one case modeled on Versailles and in the other on Spanish Romanesque examples.

"All normal life, kitchens, lavatories, all the *stage machinery* is relegated to the cellars.

"Gradually, he forces the servants to appear masked when they have to wait on him; at Lindenhof, he has a table that disappears through the floor of the closet by mechanical means when the meal is finished.

"The rest is mirrors, ivory, Chinese vases clinging like alpinists to high baroque shelves beneath ceilings where neo-Raphaelite angels and *putti* chase each other toward twilight clouds.

"But mirrors above all, mirrors, silver-coated masterpieces of mirrors that deepen each room endlessly, repeating the gold and the stucco until you get dizzy."

"So Ludwig never got a chance to enter his own life?"

"My God, how you must have suffered to become so wise, little girl," said the professor appreciatively. "Precisely. He was trapped in the *image* of a lifestyle, trapped in the common idea of royalty, of Versailles, of King Arthur's court, and trapped there forever in such a way that of course he never had a chance to become King Ludwig.

"He is, so to speak, a king whose whole fame consists of the fact that he tried to be something else."

"Possibly with *one exception*, if you'll allow: the dark and stormy night by the shore of the Starnbergersee, when he strangles his attendant psychiatrist and then himself disappears in the waves."

"It's all a story of a *consumer*, isn't it?"

"Of course. He used up tremendous amounts of *the best*. The best marble: the black. The best ivory: the white. Gold leaf. Only silvered mirrors, mirrors with silver wire, would do. Of course, he kept tens of thousands of artisans occupied and raised the level of Bavarian crafts."

"The first consumer? The first suburbanite? The first holder of a Diner's Club card? The first one to make a concerted effort to *live inside the image* instead of . . . "

"Yes, instead of what?"

This last was said by the woman, quite surprisingly. She was engaged in a careful inspection of her inside left thigh, looking for something that might be a dangerous mosquito bite, perhaps malarial.

This distracted both of her companions to the bursting point.

"Don't worry, probably it's just me who did it," he said, putting an arm across her shoulders. She immediately shrugged it off.

She was seriously disturbed by this conversation.

"*Consumer*," he said. "O.K. *Someone who lives inside the image of a lifestyle* and who himself equals zero. But there are other possible analyses."

"Which ones?" Professor Jantz asked. (He still felt rather excited by this business of the inside white thigh.) There were little, downy, golden hairs that showed up very plainly right now, when the sun had worked through a gap in the voluminous clouds.

"Oh, I imagine him on a cold, dark Bavarian autumn day, sitting by his leaded window, looking out across two valleys and the distant lake, *knowing that he's nothing in particular*. Naturally, that's what's making him vain, dreamy, and devoted to splendiferous display to an absolutely mad degree: he is the first Wittelsbach without any qualities.

"Of course, he almost has to go under when Wagner leaves him.

"He sits there, looking out over the autumnal valley where scarcely a single leaf remains. The sky is gray, the pack of carefully selected Pomeranians is barking in the kennels, and he can hear it all the way up here, by the leaded window. He's sitting by his leaded window, watching a flock of black crows whirling across the valley, and he is literally nothing. . . "

"What do you mean by that?" the woman asked. "Don't you want to swim back? I feel like a drink."

"I mean that perhaps it was all simply *a way of surviving November*."

"Now what do you mean?"

"I mean that *a way of surviving November* is necessary in everybody's life. It's an art, isn't it? God, how trivial he was, this Bavarian king!"

4

Professor Jantz had scheduled the seminar on Jekyll Island for a particular reason.

He needed to swim, for the sake of his circulation.

He had been here before: he knew how to appreciate water that stayed at almost 70 degrees far into November.

He started swimming well before breakfast every morning. His wife, tall, skinny, very well groomed, always accompanied him on these swims.

At eleven o'clock, just before lunch, it was time again. And then an equally long swim in the afternoon.

These Germans with their fanatic national preoccupation with their own bodies, their circulatory problems, their health institutes, their liver cures, their incessant fussing over their own bodies, autoerotic yet impersonal, sometimes got on his nerves. He ran into it so often at conferences and on trips.

It was difficult to decide what significance it had.

Were they engaged in a subtle kind of pleasure? Or was this some price that had to be paid for something else, a price beyond the freeways, the Mercedes Benzes, the beautiful white alpine houses in Tessin?

It was an almost interminable, desolate shore they swam along. Evidently, Professor Jantz and his wife never talked to each other when they were swimming. The American woman was jocular when she got into the water, swam on her back for long stretches and pointed at the numbers of pelicans out in the surf, which intensified as the day wore on.

The hotel vanished rapidly; soon you could only see the beach, and one point of land was just like the next.

One day, they had found a rotting seal: it was lying among the rocks, buzzing with flies, half covered by strange tropical leeches, or things that, to his eyes, looked like tropical leeches. A large, heavy, rotting body which somehow *had* to capture their attention.

After inspecting it carefully, and after exclaiming at the stench—the repugnant, offensive smell of decomposition which could only have been annihilated by putting it on a fire and letting it burn; the American woman had even poked it with a stick (and discovered that it went right through the soft sealskin if she wanted it to)—they had retreated westward, back toward the hotel beach.

The strange thing was that nobody really felt like swimming any more.

It was an extremely interesting beach: just the way in which wind and sand shaped the silver-colored wood was enough to occupy your fancy for hours. And the shells at low tide with their strange left- and right-hand whorls, the same shell in every way imaginable, every little detail, every speck of color the same—but, and it was a difference that was the whole difference, so to speak—where one had left-hand whorls the other's turned inexorably in the opposite direction.

As if the one had traveled through the universe and returned at last, here, to its beach, to find the other one, which had always been here.

After lunch they resumed deliberations. He left the American woman—she was just about to immerse herself in the fourth thick paperback novel of the week (altogether identical to the earlier ones), just purchased at the newsstand in the low, bungalowlike reception building at the hotel—they all seemed to be about the same tremendous passion which blew like a trade wind through the even thickness of the paperback novels on American newsstands.

They continued their discussion, and a totally bald man from New York summarized a paper that dealt with finding entirely new ways of describing economic conditions in times when economic conditions are no longer stabile.

All of it was terribly uncertain and verbal, and for some years now, he'd had the feeling that seminars like this one wouldn't be held much longer.

It wasn't possible to talk reality out of reality, and neither the violent riots reported on the TV screen now from this, now that Third World country, nor the violently fluctuating exchange rates could be kept in place by theoretical constructions made by experts of the '50s who had had the simple, the all too simple, task of predicting what would happen if growth were to continue.

In his highly industrialized home country, it was no longer economically feasible to carry out proper snow removal in the winter, or for a single working-class family to have steak or any other meat.

The bottom had fallen out of the highly industrialized world, and here a few people were sitting on a beach talking.

While others went swimming for the sake of their circulation, and some encountered grand passion in paperbacks.

Tomorrow he would drive the American woman to Jacksonville. Her plane for Boston (God only knew what she would do in Boston, but Boston was where she wanted to go) left very early, and he would have to sit half the day at the airport with a book. And there certainly wasn't much he objected to about that.

He had the feeling that if he stayed for a few more days by himself, he would be drawn into the relationship between the German professor and his silent, discreetly obedient wife, that he would be forced into a role as some kind of *witness* between two people who were actually engaged in a subtle life-and-death struggle, and that this role as *witness* would distract him, torment him, and take up his time for several weeks.

They all said goodbye to one another warmly, almost extravagantly, in the parking lot in front of the reception building.

The professor intended to stay another two weeks and attend to his circulation.

There was very little traffic on the road, which mostly ran through mangroves once he got onto the mainland.

Lightly, he said goodbye to the American woman when her flight was announced in Jacksonville. She waved gaily with her cosmetics case and the paperback about *passion*, which she hadn't quite finished.

He couldn't help laughing out loud—from a kind of joy that such things existed. With light steps, he went to the snack bar to order a large cup of coffee.

There would still be time to call home and tell them that he figured on arriving back on the transatlantic flight in about eighteen hours.

He had the feeling that he'd lived through one of those novels that never come into being, simply because while all the ingredients are there, no one dares put them into too close a contact with one another.

5

Oh these mountains that only bring forth mice!

He returned on a Friday in November. It was obvious that there was snow in the air: he guessed it would start falling any time now, there was the tell-tale dryness.

He arrived on the three o'clock train. There was no point in renting a car at Arlanda, no hurry any more.

Nobody was home when he got there. Consequently, he sat down in the kitchen, as visible as possible from the driveway; if his wife had someone with her when she came home, she ought to have a chance to see that he was there, in order to avoid unpleasant surprises.

Instead of turning up with a lover, she failed to appear at all.

He sat there hour after hour. The furnace hummed a bit, and he felt vaguely like checking to see what mail might be waiting for him, but when it came to the point, he found he didn't really feel like it; there wouldn't be anything but bills and invitations to other conferences anyway, and they no longer appealed to him in the least.

If he only knew where the hell she'd gone.

He seriously considered calling around, to some friends and relations, but he decided against it.

It's so easy to make a fool of yourself.

He had a couple of whiskeys and went to bed.

It was absolutely impossible to go to sleep. There was a pain in his gut, and it wasn't the usual manifestation of emptiness; it was something else, not crying, crying would have been too childish, but rather crying in its crystallized form. Feelings have a tendency of their own to become *banal* just before they burst.

He wasn't able to *find his way back* to the love he must once have felt for her. The odds and ends in the kitchen, the traces of her pottering with the plants in the window—she must have left quite recently—everything said to him that he must have loved her once, and instead he had to invent *something else*.

Like Lucia in the mad scene in Donizetti's opera *Lucia di Lammermoor*. She has been betrayed; the whole world, even the winds and the mountains, have betrayed her in the shape of a perfidious love, and she cannot find the way back to her love.

She finds something else, something ridiculous, something parodic or banal instead. A fragment from a hit tune instead of the great song.

And that doesn't last very long, naturally.

Oh these mountains that bring forth nothing but mice.

The next morning there was no wind; it was cold, with dry snow underfoot. He had gone to sleep around six, and just as he was falling asleep he remembered that she was supposed to be away for two weeks, on a charter flight to Rhodes with a woman friend.

He pulled on shoes, sweat suit, gloves.

He ran out into the dry November air; it was right before a new snowfall; he was running calmly and rhythmically, and he no longer knew what he was running from.

The Girl in the Blue Cap

It wasn't insomnia in the usual sense of the word: rather, it was a flaw, a place where his sleep had broken once and for all and could no longer be repaired. It was between three and four in the morning. He called it his "sleep injury," and he knew exactly when and how it had occurred.

But that's another story.

In any case, there it was, more pronounced in December and January, months when he was always tired and depressed, less so than in the spring—he had a hard time tolerating too much darkness.

As the years go by, someone who has a gap like that in his sleep will acquire something resembling a secret life.

The sleepless hour was *completely* sleepless: it possessed all the shadowless, labyrinthine clarity of total, absolute sleeplessness, like a desert city in Mexico or a high plateau in the Alps where an unmerciful light never ceases to shine.

Or perhaps like one of those science-fiction planets that has two suns; when one sets red on the horizon the other one rises on the opposite horizon, conferring a terrifying, bluish light on the new day.

If he neglected his injury, he had to lie there sleepless until morning and then live through an awful day with a headache that started early in the afternoon. Neglecting it meant too much of the whole thing. If you just treated it like the most natural thing in the world, you would begin to feel, at a quarter of or ten to four, how the landscape, dried out by that awful clarity, started to fill with the waters of sleepiness; the gentle rain of tiredness would fill the stony, parched creek beds in the landscape of your soul, and all of a sudden, you were back among normal people: you slept, as soundly as a child.

There were different things you could do during this empty

hour: but it was essential to endure its merciless, dry light—its wakefulness.

At home, he was careful never to use this secret hour for work. Thinking about your problems was dangerous. You would always find new ones. Reading novels was impossible. There was always the risk that you would find the novel so interesting that you continued reading past four o'clock.

Something like the *Encyclopèdia Britannica* was ideal. Not the recent one, which was mostly a reference work, but the nice old one, with its long, comprehensive articles on subjects no one knew anything about nowadays, *Kufic coins, Edward's Plateau.* Anything would do in the eleventh or twelfth edition. *Le Grande Larousse* wasn't bad, either.

It isn't easy, though, to lug obsolete editions of heavy encyclopedias around the world.

He was an experimental physicist and had contracts with various international organizations, mostly those who had extraordinary research facilities at their disposal: CERN in Switzerland, the Tokama reactor at the University of Texas, the linear accelerator at Stanford.

It often takes six to eight months to set up even a minor project in experimental physics. (Magnifying glasses are cheap—microscopes already a bit higher. X-ray crystallography is something that requires days of preparation. *Magnification is expensive* and *the cost of further magnification increases logarithmically,* he used to tell his children when occasionally they showed some interest—to them, nuclear physics was already an obsolete occupation, something that belonged to a world which, no matter what, wouldn't be able to afford sending daddies around the world in airplanes much longer, and that was just as well. The children themselves were mostly interested in indoor plants, organic salads, and Bach sonatas: they were involved in what, during his high school years, had been typical interests for girls.)

In the sleeplessness of hotel rooms, he had acquired the habit of reading telephone books. Like the hotel Bible, which for some reason he avoided like the plague, they were always available.

But telephone books were fun. You could see that the watchmakers in New Delphi, in spite of the size of the city, were concentrated in an area of less than a square mile. You could also see that Houston had more entries for *Olsen* than for *Olson*; that there was an abundance of people called Dürrenmatt in Zürich, but that the real Dürrenmatt, that is to say the playwright, did not have his name in the book.

You could see, or rather infer, the statistical population distribution: you could see to what extent people were interchangeable, how far the degree of diffusion, entropy, similarity of quality had gone; in foreign continents, almost like the faint traces of vapor in a Wilson cloud chamber, the traces of a European past that no longer existed. The Lettish names in the Chicago telephone book. The memories from Lodz and Lublin on the Stanford campus. The last traces of General Vlassov's Ukranian rebel army, the one that joined Hitler's cause and turned against the Soviet Union in 1942, all existed like Wilson traces in Sidney telephone books as Ukranian groceries, Ukranian hairdressers.

Now he was in Göteborg, actually to discuss a matter concerning a research council with Professor Karl Erik Eriksson, but also to inspect a sailboat dry-docked in Kungsbacka (this happened in the middle of February of 1977) that an acquaintance had called him about. For a long time he'd been looking for a small sailboat, but it was difficult. The price rose so rapidly that every time he'd put some money aside, the boat was already more expensive than he could afford.

He had a rather large house in Lidingö. Taxwise, this was not as good as it had been.

It had not been difficult to come to an agreement with Professor Eriksson, small, mercurial, sharp-witted and skeptical, but it had proved absolutely impossible to track down the man with the sailboat. According to a friend of a friend, he was still living in Kungsbacka. But at the number where the man was supposed to be, or at least was supposed to have been last summer, he was told that the telephone was no longer in service.

The ridiculous thing is that in such a situation, you don't feel you can very well ask for an explanation. Hadn't he paid his bill, had he gone bankrupt, or had he perhaps died?

46

What happens if you ask? Presumably, you don't get an answer.

So he'd called around to people he'd heard were friends of the man with the boat, *Hans-Åke Ohlson,* and he had talked to a jazz pianist, a professor of theoretical philosophy specializing in medieval, so-called "terministic" logic, very entertaining and pleasant, and to a nice lady whose husband worked in what was left of the ship-building industry up there. Nice people on the whole, but not a single one had the faintest idea about *Hans-Åke Ohlson* with the boat and his whereabouts.

Hans-Åke Ohlson, with an "h" and one "s."

Now it was late at night; he woke up between three and four and reached for the phone book. In Göteborg there are two books, and since the second one happened to be on top on his bedside table, he was soon engrossed in the letter "N." Surprisingly, lots of Yugoslav names, especially Croatian ones, start with an "N."

Lots of *Nyström*'s and, surprisingly, a *Julia Nyström,* something which is apt to surprise someone who knows that Julia Nyström was the daughter of a foundry owner from Skultuna in Västmanland and who, at the height of Romanticism, wrote one of the immortal poems of the period, "Fresh Winds of Spring."

Or was that a mistake? Suddenly he felt very uncertain—and at 3:18 on a February night in Götborg, the opportunity for checking a fact of literary history is not very great, nor other facts, either, as far as that's concerned. He was preparing to go on to another letter when he found *Ann-Marie Nöme.*

That name is really unusual. It seems like a name someone has made up, if not in this generation than in the previous one, when people still had a snobbish interest in what they were called.

But that wasn't what captivated his interest.

He had known a girl with that name, at the end of junior high and his first year of high school. And he was quite sure that she was dead.

He had been very fond of her; he had gone out with her for a while. A blonde, rather small, if he remembered correctly a very musical girl, very warm, a great aptitude for kissing. In some indefinable way, fragile. They used to go to the school dances—it must have been the winter of 1952 or 1953; at that time, they always had to have a Dixieland band. The girls either in dresses or else sweaters with gray or black, sometimes blue, pleated skirts. You pressed close to each other, investigated each other, you might say, without daring very much in those days.

Those of his classmates who really had a relationship with a girl were few and easily became heroes.

She was great. He remembered her in the snow. He often made a date to meet her downtown. For some reason he no longer remembered, he disliked picking her up at her parents' home; maybe he was scared of her parents.

For that reason, he remembered her standing in some kind of winter coat, waiting in new-fallen snow outside a store, a jewelry store with a big, heavy clock hanging over the sidewalk. That's where he used to meet her.

He didn't know or couldn't remember what she had died from, or perhaps he had never known.

On the other hand, he remembered his two or three visits to the hospital. She was very thin then, almost emaciated, in a hospital gown made from a coarse fabric; he remembered the rough feel of it around her wrist when he—now with a slight feeling of repulsion—bent across the pillow and gingerly kissed her forehead.

(Nowadays, he had the feeling of not really loving anybody, not the way he had been able to love people when he was young. And it was safer this way.)

At any rate: a pale March light had shone on her where she lay, in rather bad shape, alone in a room in the massive, old, barracks-like hospital which then existed in his hometown. The flowers he had brought were yellow, daffodils perhaps. He didn't remember a whole lot. Yes, a faint smell of chemicals, hospital smells, her thin, sort of waxy face. There couldn't have been many hospital visits.

In quantum physics, it is a basic assumption that only an observed phenomenon could be considered a phenomenon.

But for this reason the universe, in some mysterious way, was dependent on its observers, or at any rate on their experimental equipment. Suppose that two currents of electrons pass through two narrow slits and are captured on a photographic plate. You will then get a pattern of dots where the quantum waves from the two slits reinforce each other and empty space where they extinguish each other.

But which electrons came from which pile is something you'll never know.

The uncomfortable thing was that the same universe had to have a beginning and an end. Something had to exist inside that huge funnel surrounded by the gates of time, its beginning and end. And could what existed in there simply consist of disjunctions, of alternatives, of entirely different possibilities? Did the universe consist of its own observers, of its own experimental arrangements?

Did the world simply consist of someone observing it? But without a world, there wouldn't be any observers.

Was a human being something along the lines of the sun's reflections on swiftly moving water? Something that became visible at a certain angle, invisible from another?

Nobody knows what a human being is, clever Pascal wrote in his "Essay on Empty Space." Because as distinct from animals, with their limited perfection, human beings have unlimited possibilities for development.

In every direction?

He had never cared much for hotel breakfasts, possibly with the exception of those in Swiss hotels, with their hot, rich bread, their heavy, white, starched napkins. Or the hotels in the American South, with their strange, baroque breakfasts: sausages, pancakes, smoked oysters, and fruit mingled together in an Arcimboldi world.

This hotel offered a typical hotel breakfast: something *pretending* to be substantial, pretending to be excellent, but which was only a dry, artificially rich, uninteresting industrial product. He had a hard time understanding why people living in great consumer societies had such difficulty in seeing that they were being cheated as consumers, too. They were told that they were living in luxury, but as a matter of fact, it was impossible for everyone to have access to quality products. They lived in a world of packaging, surrounded by objects that pretended they were desirable but were not.

As a member of society, he was trapped in a refraction pattern, a huge, shimmering carpet of sun reflections which would disappear, leaving only emptiness behind the minute you moved the observer a fraction of an inch to either side.

It would disappear the way a school of minnows, in the spring, disappears in the shallows when the shadow of a passer-by falls across the water.

After breakfast, he got a telephone call telling him that his business had gotten fouled up. *Hans-Åke Ohlson* with the boat had actually gotten in touch. He would call back that afternoon. And the physicists would not finish their proposals until tomorrow. Sitting in his room with the *Svenska Dagbladet* in his lap, feeling momentarily empty, he reached for the telephone book.

Resolutely, he called *Ann-Marie Nöme.*

As the phone was ringing, he was struck by the madness of his enterprise.

Can you say to a total stranger: "Excuse me, but I'm conducting an experiment; I'd like to know if you're dead.

"Or if you're somebody else whom I don't know."

Sufficiently curious, sufficiently excited and amused by his own fantasy, he jotted down the address on a piece of paper and took a cab. It was a cold, clear day in late winter, and the sky—something which does not always happen in Göteborg—was absolutely blue and clear. They drove through streets that became more and more quiet, toward the oak forest and the gently rolling hills and little lakes around the West Hospital.

He had deliberately given the driver the wrong number so that he would be able to walk the last stretch. He paid and got out, thinking: "Of course it's a crazy idea, an absolutely idiotic idea, but I'll get some fresh air, and I'll get some sunshine, some contact with nature. It's good to see large trees, still bare, with snow in their branches."

The snow was thicker and cleaner out here, shoveled into proper banks along the street; the houses were small and quite well kept; here and there, the built-up areas were interrupted by areas of parkland—it was what's called a well-planned and esthetically appealing suburb.

The temperature in the city proper was just at the freezing point; here it must be a couple of degrees below that: his cheeks were tingling. The suburbs and the city centers often differ from each other this way.

"Excuse me, I'm conducting an experiment."

"Oh?"

"Either you're identical with a person with the same name. And in that case, you're dead. Or else you are different from the one who is dead, and in that case you're alive."

No matter how hard he thought, it was impossible to come up with a sensible beginning to that kind of conversation.

He walked along the street with slow, embarrassed steps. How was he going to find another cab out here?

He looked around for a phone booth, and when he glanced up again, he saw her.

There was no doubt that it was she. Every detail fit; there was no possibility of a misunderstanding. In that case, it would have to be a twin sister who had been kept secret for decades, a thought he dismissed as too nineteenth century.

Blonde, strong, a little rounder, a little middle-aged, with red cheeks, dressed in a black fur coat and blue knitted cap, she came out from between the stone gateposts and turned on to his side of the street. With short cries of command, she directed two strong, supple Labradors in front of her. They seemed extremely happy to be let out for a walk with their mistress and rolled ecstatically in the new snow under the oaks in the park.

51

When they got quite close to each other, she peered at him short-sightedly; for an instant there was a look of surprise, of half-recognition, of almost embarrassed wondering in her eyes.

He solved the problem for her by doffing his hat politely and giving her the most dazzling smile he was capable of.

She returned his greeting just as warmly, just as confusedly, and disappeared down the street.

On his way to the bus stop, he realized that he was either at the beginning or at the end of a very powerful story.

He hoped fervently that *Hans-Åke Ohlson,* the man who wanted to sell his sailboat, would turn up today as well.

What Does Not Kill Us,
Tends to Make Us Stronger

1

Through the humid, surprisingly warm February air, the heavy, humid February spring of the Southern states, he ran ten thousand meters, swam for a short while in a swimming pool constructed in a clear creek at the outskirts of town, and headed back through the thickening morning traffic almost without seeing another human being.

Mornings like this one he could still feel an ecstatic joy at being in America, even after many years. America protected him, wrapped him in warm Southern air as in a blanket, America fed him with her pale beers and her funny, incomprehensible TV shows. America had saved him, once and for all, by giving him tenure at a Southern university, to lecture forever on Swedish Art Nouveau, on the poetry of Oscar Levertin, on art in the Thiel Art Gallery, on the renaissance of Verner von Heidenstam, on "Pepita's Wedding" and "The Daughter of Jairus."

The 1890s were the high point and crest of Swedish literature, and the wonderful Swedish *fin de siècle* could really only survive with him, here in America.

He had arrived as far back as 1957—after a thesis defense at what was then called Stockholms Högskola, which hadn't quite gone the way he had hoped; he had more or less built Scandinavian Studies from the ground up at his university, built it from an old Germanic Languages Department filled with dusty volumes of Goethe, dominated by Germans in exile, already getting old, who had recommendations dating from the Allied Control Commission in Berlin, which was dispensing with their interpreters just about that time. They had worked quite well together, those somewhat eccentric Germans who mostly seemed to live for Gothic and Old High German vowel shifts, and he had found coexistence easy: they were people in exile, although of a different kind, a species who could not harm one another, people who could get along and survive in approximately the same ecological environment without much conversation.

His thesis defense had taken place on one of the final days of May 1957—he still didn't like to think about it. During the break, it was already obvious that he would not be offered a teaching post, and a few days later, while the Grading Committee deliberated, he had almost gone mad.

There were rumors that perhaps his thesis wouldn't even pass.

Then it did; he spent a difficult summer, and at the end of August that year, 1957, right in the heat of August, in the dog days when nobody goes outside. (He didn't even know how to drive a car then; he wouldn't even have managed to buy groceries if a kindly female assistant professor of German, a nice, absent-minded Jewish woman from New York, hadn't adopted him. She'd died many years ago, of cancer, by the way.) At that time, he had had a temporary job as a research assistant, having to do with some kind of exchange with the Sweden-America Foundation, and the idea was that he'd stay for a semester. But at the end of the semester, he'd wangled an extension; he didn't quite have the nerve to return after what a rival had written in his review of the dissertation in *Dagens Nyheter*. In the meantime, a teaching assistant had fallen sick. He had been somewhat afraid of the students for the first few weeks, before he discovered that they were actually fascinated by his teaching—they'd never run across a teacher who spoke about literature in a similar manner.

And so it had continued, and he hadn't even returned for the separate funerals of his parents.

A tenure-track job, with tenure after only five years. He'd probably never be a full professor, because now, in the '70s, it was harder to get promoted, and in 1977 he'd been here for twenty years.

And last winter his wife had died.

54

He ran through the heavy, humid air, which would eventually develop into rain, and he enjoyed it immensely.

> *I, Bernal Diaz del Castillo, citizen and governor of the most loyal city of Santiago de Guatemala, speak of what concerns me and all true Conquistadors, my companions who served His Majesty the King by discovering, pacifying, and colonizing most of the provinces of New Spain: and that this is the best land so far discovered in the New World which we found by our own efforts, without His Majesty knowing anything of it.*

There were always high points. Moments when he could see quite clearly that Greatness begins in meaninglessness, that every great plan carries its own death within, and that we are born and renewed every moment we are capable of abandoning ourselves.

The remarkable thing, of course, is that a series of runs like that, three or four mornings in a row, almost always deal with the same thing. You think it, you almost dream it, as you run.

Then you forget it all day. And the next morning, there it is, back again.

We don't dream only at night. All wise people—no, that's putting it too strongly—but *some* wise people know that there are dreams that glide in front of your eyes when you're wide-awake.

But they have no chance of becoming visible, as little as stars in the daytime. They become transparent instead.

That's what happens: they become *transparent.*

Transparent dreams had hovered about him ever since his wife's death. She was a girl from Houston, and since his own childhood had transpired around Humlegården and Karlaplan in Stockholm, they had had an almost secret agreement not to speak much with each other about their childhoods.

(On the whole, their relationship had been very polite.)

Now that she was gone, it was as if some mild prohibition had been lifted. It had hovered around all winter: now it was the smell of elder, the giant bird-cherry bush at the crest of the Vitaberg Park, a waterfall of white blossoms looking out over the city and the water, beauty from the early years of the '50s, an abiding beauty in the Stockholm of the '50s which had disappeared forever, that only existed here with him, on his lonely run.

The smell of the big bird-cherry bushes. The smell of elder and of lilac. The smell of blacktop in the schoolyard.

In a way, it all meant schoolyard.

Confounded cruelty! Schoolyard in June. The school is closed, only the cleaning women are there, dragging their heavy buckets.

The smell of dry chalkdust mingled with the smell from the lives of flowers, of trees.

And of course: the school is closed because the grades have already been given.

In the midst of this waking dream, just as he had reached the point where he turned around and swung onto something called Shoal Creek Boulevard, a sudden, unruly gust of wind blew in from Riddarfjärden, making the sailboats keel deep in the Stockholm of the '50s, drawing the smoke from the chimneys in the central city into long streamers in the wind.

He was on his way home again. And above him this Southern sky, blue as the sky in Mallarmé's poem "L'Azur," an intoxicating blue emptiness that you might fall into if you weren't careful.

Now he cut across lawns and bushes, up toward Fifth Street, leaving the large park area behind, and could already feel the traffic fouling the air he breathed. Now he was in a black part of town, blacks everywhere, small, improvised wooden houses, often refrigerators and rusting old cars in the yard, bikes and lawnmowers rusting together in brotherly consort, all the modern world's crazy paraphernalia of meaningless technological products, designed to keep people calm and convinced that they were involved in something meaningful. He was living in meaningless times.

Several of the blacks in the small houses greeted him in a friendly way. He ran past here so often in the mornings on his way to the university that they had started to view him as part of the natural happenings of their morning.

He passed the big traffic lights on Fourth Street. Now the tower of the university library came into sight.

Here he would always think of Bernal Diaz: "*When we had*

passed this headland we were on the high seas. . . ." It had such a marvelous ring.

> *When we had passed this headland we were on the high seas; trusting to fortune we steered toward the setting sun, knowing nothing about the depth of the water, nor of currents, nor of the winds which generally prevail at this latitude, so that our lives were in great peril when a storm struck us, lasting for two days and two nights, raging with such force that we were nearly lost."*

Something he often thought about was what Saint-John Perse had called "time crests," the experience of finding yourself in a civilization at the moment when it reaches its fullest development, when its most secret energies come into bloom. France at the time of Racine's plays. Pascal starts publishing his first mathematical treatises, for example the one that tells you how to calculate the volume of a staircase, nothing else, just how to calculate the volume of a staircase, and at the same time it encompasses all of Pascal, the clarity, the azure blue sky which no passions can disturb, only despair and clarity and for the rest, silence.

In the cloister of Port-Royal, Arnaud and Nicole write their logic together, a crystal-clear homage to reason, a completely empty and happy book, which believes that there can be no more surprises (the really happy epochs always believe that the time of surprises is past). But still full, like a seed pod, of the possibilities for another time, already pregnant with the possibilities which must lead to the fall of classicism.

It won't be long before Port-Royal has to close, the discussion is transformed into orthodoxy, and silence; the Jansenists banished from conversation, the splendor of the court ballets fades, the police state closes its rusty iron doors, shutting out the light of reason.

The light in the mirrors will have a fainter brilliance. The smell of dirt from the dungeons of the imprisoned will penetrate the halls of mirrors, the smell of the beggers' rags will be carried from their dirty, closed-in alleys, and the summer wind, already sick, will bring them into gardens where philosophers move in slow, ambulating conversation with court ladies.

"Oh what a shame, the wind is from the South end today."

2

The department was small. This didn't prevent it from developing a great, labyrinthine inner life.

There were specialists in German, Dutch, Yiddish, Norwegian, Old Norse, and yes, there was an old gentleman who had come from the University of Århus right after the war and who still, at least once every academic year, arranged a very detailed and tedious seminar on the tales of Hans Christian Andersen. He was an inoffensive man who had started to look a bit like a nice old fairy-tale uncle himself. He had white sideburns that rolled down his cheeks like treble clefs and round, red cheeks.

Traditionally, the German professors were well off—some of them had been in the diplomatic corps in their younger days, and some, as has already been mentioned, belonged to the old employees of the Allied Control Commission. German was snobbish. The Scandinavian languages were more something for madmen, a hobby that all of a sudden might engage pimply young men who still lived at home with mother.

Of course, there was also a division between radicals and conservatives that had existed for a decade, no, actually for much longer. There were the Brecht specialists and the young research assistants who had written their dissertations on Kluge and Enzensberger and visited Berlin in the '60s, and there were the conservatives, particularly well represented among the linguists. The conservatives were in the majority, and consequently they tried to prevent the young Marxists from getting tenure whenever they could. This never went too far, however, since everyone knew that they might be paid back when the positions of his own friends or protégés were at stake at the close of some other semester.

The chairman was a gentle, quiet translator with a taste for fine suits. He had been chosen because of his insignificance. It was more important to know that one of the female professors had once been married to a member of the university administration and that one of the most radical of the German professors played raquetball every Thursday with the dean of the College of Liberal

Arts, which comprised three disciplines and controlled a budget of hundreds of millions.

It was a fairly simple game; you learned it in two semesters, and only crazy men, neurotics who insisted on some extra suffering and very stupid people, did not learn it. He himself considered both conservatism and Marxism as subtopics in the introductory fall courses on the history of ideas in the nineteenth century, too conservative actually to be interested in either.

There was a stink of industrialism, of freeways, of cheap motels with the smell of smoke in the sheets, around all political debate. He reserved to himself the right to insist that only great epochs could have politics. At best, epochs like this one could have election campaigns, offers that in no way differed from the soap commercial campaigns on TV.

Shvitzbuden, an old Jewish invention, dating from the time of Masada or King David, are something you only find at American universities and, like private institutions full of cigar-smoking gentlemen, in a few streets in Chicago and New York.

Shvitzbuden are, as you can almost deduce from the name, much wetter than saunas; the air is fed with steam, and it's very difficult to see anything for the first ten minutes inside a *Shvitzbud*.

While he pulled off his sweatsuit—it was still early enough in the year to use a sweatsuit—thoughtfully pulling the pants down over his knees, which were getting bonier and more angular every year (he could still remember the round knees of his childhood, like sweet rolls, and how they hurt when you fell down on the gravel), he knew just about what morning crew he would find in there.

Three younger mathematicians who were always discussing real-estate prices, and the new, inexpensive supermarkets along Interstate 35 they had just investigated (they had all gotten married a few years ago). One came from Chicago and two from Harvard, and all three of them were still surrounded by an aura of youth and promise and spoke of the world as if it consisted of high-salaried professorships and Bernouilli transformations.

And then that nice Bernstein from the Hebrew Department, a

59

gentle, very articulate Benjamin who was always playing raquet-ball and who often forgot to remove the sweatband from his forehead.

He knew that they would be in there, greeting him with a many-voiced hello through the fog. They would exchange the usual faculty jokes, and he knew exactly how he would answer.

What struck him more and more often was the narcissistic aspect of this whole fitness craze. For miles, tens of miles in every direction, young, middle-aged, and older men and women were jogging, biking, participating in archery, volleyball, in God knows what all, and essentially they were nothing but a blind, uncertain, narcissistic generation preoccupied with the last and, in its own way, the most fragile of all the continents of hope: your own body.

There was no point at which people hadn't stopped hoping. Nowadays, the problem of the slums was handled with theft insurance and an increasing tendency toward the establishment of ghettos: residents of different parts of town no longer visited each other. With faintly liberal, therapeutic formulations, they tried to hide the fact that evil was considered as inevitable, crime and violence as the basic conditions of society, on which the law and the state could only impose its sanctions like an uncertain, winding mosaic in the original rock.

Industrialism was viewed as a necessary evil, no, as a rockslide which nothing could prevent any longer; its products had long since ceased to fascinate them (anyway, around eighty percent were military products which no one would ever see unless the ultimate happened) and were viewed as toys, designed essentially to keep the slum dwellers in a good mood and give them something to fight for.

You yourself had your body, the deep feeling of inhaling, of well-being, of deep muscular peace after a ten-mile run.

Your body was your castle, your own territory, a fortress against an essentially indifferent environment (yes, there was sex as well, but good God, everyone knows that it's either limited or else, if you make it unlimited, it dooms you to loss of identity, to passivity, slavery, and yes, forgetting the world).

60

But your body had many kinds of significance: it wasn't just a fortress against your environment, it was also the first, the most immediate form of environment you encountered.

The only one you could control. And the only one you could lose.

Your body was the only area of the world where multiple significance was the rule.

That's why you had to run.

With a very slow, very conscious, almost esthetically conscious movement, he pushed the heavy door open and entered the boiling hot, maternal fog of the room. Five voices shouted, "Hello, Lars," as on command.

It wasn't even nine o'clock. True reality wouldn't start for another half-hour.

3

Home at three, he parked the car carelessly, at an angle in front of the garage, took the morning paper lying in its plastic wrapper where the paper boy had thrown it in the dry grass. And it struck him that the lawn needed a thorough going-over. Small, round balls of Spanish moss had blown from the pecan trees during the storms in December and January—midwinter in Texas never ceased to amaze him: it was so abstract.

A bit empty, a bit absent-minded, but not at all unfriendly.

It was like a very absent-minded soul.

In the morning it's about 40 to 45 degrees; then the temperature might rise to 60 or even 65 in the afternoon, except on windy days.

Huge flocks of sparrows come from the south, more and more birds every day. The waxwings settle in the cedars; the doves coo softly in the gardens; a flock of sparrows rises in a half-whirl over the plains. These flocks of sparrows often look like the souls dancing around in Doré's wood engravings for Dante's *Inferno*, the way he had seen them as a child—there was something disquieting about them.

If you got out on the big interstates, 45 to Houston or 35 to San

Antonio, you could see what a lot of birds gathered in whirls like that at this time of year. So much wind, such a sea of air: the empty reflection of the big blizzards always raging in the north at this time of year.

A kind of abstract blizzard without snow.

Such days he remembered how softly the snow had fallen on Östermalm in the '50s, what it would feel like to walk from Karlaplan to Humlegården on an evening in the beginning of December, no, not evening, it must have been in the afternoon, early afternoon when the streetlights are lit. And big, heavy snowflakes falling one by one.

He had known a girl on 45 Karlavägen in those days. She lived with her father and sister in a large, gloomy apartment on the fourth floor; sometimes you would catch a glimpse of a silent, formal maidservant in the entry hall. At that time, the end of the '50s, people must still have had maidservants on Östermalm.

He even remembered the dry, very clean, sort of well-mannered smell in such apartments; the whole atmosphere when you were asked to a dinner dance, those ladies in black who took your coat.

The girls' long dresses with very wide belts.

Didn't they use to have very wide belts?

Or was that just in the spring?

He liked those dances in someone's home very much. His own father was a widower too (as he was now, himself, and at the same age, it suddenly occurred to him)—but his apartment was much too small for such things. His father was the head of a department in the Finance Office, a quiet lawyer without many qualities, who invited colleagues for bridge about once a month; he didn't object to the boys he was so proud of, once they were in their last years of high school, coming in for a whiskey.

But just one, of course. Only when he did his military service, when he ended up out in Solna with the Signal Corps and made friends from other parts of town, did he realize how much of Stockholm he had missed during his high school years. A popular dancing place like Nalen on Regeringsgatan only existed for him in the form of funny ads in the *Dagens Nyheter* once a week.

And he was surprised when his buddies would lie in bed in the barracks at night, telling of all the fun bars on Söder, where it seemed they used to drop in Saturday nights. They lived in a different world, with different girls.

His beat as a high school boy was restricted. To the west, it ran from the City Library on Sveavägen, and to the east as far as Lidingö, where he also knew some girls and went to Saturday dances a few times a semester. It was a nuisance to have a girl on Lidingö. You had to keep track of the reddish-brown trains from Humlegården at night, and if you forgot yourself out there, the cab back to town could be quite expensive.

Under the round sphere of the City Library—cupola couldn't be the right word—he could sit endlessly after school—only a couple of sandwiches in passing, a quick visit to Augusta Jansson to find a kind of caramel devastating for your teeth but very good to chew on while you were reading.

There was a great deal that could engross you. Cleanth Brooks and I.A. Richards and all of the New Criticism that came in for so much discussion in the *Dagens Nyheter* and which evidently riled the literature professors no end.

It was his beloved 1890s and his delight at finding the nice little mistakes in Oskar Levertin's "Ithaka" which showed that the poet had probably never been on a ship, and if he had, he hadn't been very interested in how things are done on board:

> *More strongly every day I apprehend*
> *the music urging me:*
> *echo of the evening waves that wend*
> *toward the island bay*
> *of home. I dream; across the thwart I bend.*
> *In waves the dolphins sport;*
> *the island yet unseen, its almond scent*
> *reveals that I approach.*

As early as this, when he was seventeen, under the peculiar, Egyptian rotunda of the City Library, he was struck by how helpless true art is, how exposed to its own shortcomings. Had something perfect ever managed to interest anybody?

He felt as if the Swedish 1890s had been there for all time, just waiting for him with its ships with silken sails across the gentle, blue Mediterranean, with its dreaming pages riding through deep medieval forests, the mild twilight at the Thiel Gallery (for him, Djurgården and the 1890s were one and the same), and in the midst of the world, a white dress under violet-brown birches.

That was the time when Sweden culminated for him. Yes. And during the succeeding decades he never felt quite sure whether his own youth had transpired during the 1890s or the 1950s.

Some of his weaker students, those who came from the large ranch districts of western Texas and from what is known as the Panhandle, never really unraveled it either and were too shy to ask.

Those boys were very unsure of chronology anyway—it was not a rare occurrence for you to become aware that they believed Voltaire and Darwin to be contemporaries.

Of course there were a lot of other things, too, under the peculiar cupola of the City Library: *Bonnier's Literary Magazine,* which published all the new poets: Folke Isaksson, Staffan Larsson, Sandro Key-Åberg, and whatever they were called. And at Tegner's Restaurant, Per Rådström and Lars Forssell put on a show.

Sometimes he wondered what had become of them, all those writers he had read so eagerly on spring evenings at the end of the '50s.

Harry Martinson and Eyvind Johnson had received the Nobel Prize in 1974, and he had lectured on them for a whole semester.

He had read in some periodical or other that Forssell had been elected to the Swedish Academy. But what the hell had happened to the poets of the '50s? What kind of writing was a man like Ragnar Thoursie doing these days?

The spring he was graduating, he had been going out with a girl who wanted to study at the Opera Academy and who was very musical. She was a bit shy, extremely interesting; she taught him a lot about opera, and he taught her a lot about Mahler's and Bruckner's symphonies. He used to play them on the gramophone in his room, with the funny cactus needles that were all the rage at the time.

64

You sharpened them on sandpaper; at every real crescendo or tutti they'd break off with a dull, grating sound.

They used to lie on the floor beside each other and listen, he with his arms across her hips, right where her long hair stopped.

Days when she was in the mood, he was allowed to touch her in other places, too.

They never actually managed to make love to each other, and perhaps it made no real difference.

So many words were necessary in the '50s. There were too many complicated feelings that had to be unraveled.

But they were together deep in the symphonies. You might almost say that the symphonies did it for them in a way, if only it didn't sound too cynical.

And they used to walk out to the Blockhus Point on beautiful spring Sundays, always making a long stop at the Thiel Gallery on the way back.

4

His American wife, the only wife he'd had, had been the same way, actually. Small, fragile, long-haired, with wavy, almost transparent skin like upper-class Southern girls often have. And with very large eyes.

Originally, she had taught French at Cornell.

He had purposely left everything the way it had been for as long as he remembered.

Her sewing machine still stood in a corner of the kitchen. There were also three heavy earthenware jars of pecans—they must have started to rot at the bottom of the jar long ago, and he hadn't done a thing about it.

His kitchen, as is often the case with kitchens in the South, had an exit directly into the yard, and there was her bike still, a very nice Motobecane, bought for some birthday early in the '70s, just when ten-speeds started to become really popular. The tape around the handgrips was hardly even dirty. She never used to sweat, not even during the dog days in the beginning of June when the sun stood in the sky like a fiery ball and he changed his shirt three times a day and couldn't stand to wait in the car for as long as it took for the air conditioner to get going—not even on days like those was she at all bothered by the heat.

She had possessed refinement. It expressed itself in her perfect French pronunciation, in her discreet way of dealing with other people's problems and her women friends' love affairs, and in her disapproval of loud colleagues on the faculty.

Now, afterward, it seemed to him that she had a touching trait which it took him almost fifteen years to grasp: she admired him, yes, she actually did, and he had never been able to understand why.

Just as old Greeks were useful to the Roman Empire because they represented a connection with the past, with what had been, in the same way he was useful to the huge American empire, the largest in the history of the world.

With its eight-lane highways, its huge spaceships, its armadas and its weapons, this great power was just as dependent on maintaining continuity as every empire that had existed before, and the empires of the future would in turn become equally dependent on this American empire.

With his little lectures on Scandinavian Art Nouveau in poetry and the visual arts, his seminars that barely got approved by the dean at the start of each semester because of low enrollment, he was actually a resource, a mysterious mineral without which this desolate futuristic world—which he hardly knew except in its most superficial manifestations—would not be able to exist.

You might say that his neuroses were a resource for the world he inhabited, that he was the mussel which alone, through his hurt, would produce the valuable mother-of-pearl.

And in some such way, she had been in love with him.

She had had an easy death. At an intersection at the top of a hill, her small French car had collided with a big, heavy American car. If she herself had been driving an American car the whole thing would have been a trifle, but now she was thrown out of her little Citroen and the car landed on top of her. She had died after forty minutes at the hospital.

He had heard about it on the morning news without reacting. It was not until the afternoon, when he was called to the hospital to identify her, that he had understood who it was.

As a matter of fact, traffic accidents were not that common in the city where he lived.

Death had not disfigured her. Not in any way that you couldn't overlook.

She seemed smaller than usual, that was all.

5

It was hard for him to grieve.

He missed her. Her bike stood all alone, almost reproachful in its place outside the kitchen. Nobody would ever use her sewing machine again. It had already rusted during the winter.

She would never again scold him for putting packages in the refrigerator without putting them on a plate.

He was capable of all kinds of feelings, but he felt no pain.

And those storms without snow blew through the winter.

Why was the whole world becoming so abstract?

Probably there had been a world for him once, waiting somewhere. In some mysterious way he had missed it.

His world of the 1890s with Djurgården and Waldemarsudde and the Thiel Gallery, might still exist somewhere, but not, anyhow, in the Sweden that he had left behind.

And this foreign world with its freeways, motels, nuclear airbases, and tall towers with blinking red-warning lights for incoming flights, with its raquetball courts and mastodontic libraries with electronic data retrieval whistling its way through centuries of dissertations as the shuttles of the mechanical loom had once whistled through the warps in Manchester and Liverpool, digging the grave of the old world—this whole foreign world was, literally, a new world.

The point of it often made him feel happy:
He had created his own significance.

6

Barbara, a thirty-five-year-old Jewish woman, very well educated, with a small shop where she sells antique European jewelry, calls up and asks if he wants to come along and see the first in a series of Ingmar Bergman films.

He says that he has seen so many Ingmar Bergman films, that in his youth in Stockholm you were always running to these dreary, entrancing premieres.

It doesn't help.

Barbara says that everyone discussed Bergman in seminars in the early '60s.

But what she's interested in is good old Victor Sjöström.

The one who discovered Greta Garbo once upon a time and who filmed *Herr Arne's Hoard.* And who then turns up as an old, old actor in Bergman's movies. He didn't correct her.

What did he know about Sjöström?

Not that much. That he invented the diagonal movement of people from the right-hand side of the frame to the left-hand side, which Eisenstein would later make famous in his *Ivan the Terrible.*

Film Studies was such a popular subject at his university, the courses always filled, that it was hard to get away from it.

Barbara picked him up in her big Buick, four years too old but as well cared for as if it had been a Biedermeier cabinet. She herself was elegant as always in a red coat, red umbrella, with her black hair tortured into an Afro, or an almost-Afro, a hair style that was gaining fast in popularity and which he really loathed.

Almost imperceptibly, they eased onto the freeway. Barbara was one of those American women who drive as naturally as they walk, since they'd done it since the age of thirteen. The evening traffic was already getting heavy, and the broad, rolling carpet of cars appearing behind them in the rearview mirror on the five-lane northbound city freeway engendered a feeling of festivity, of city, in him:

"Come out, my beloved, onto my balcony . . ."

The American city had a peculiarity that had scared him when he was younger, but which he had gotten used to through the years.

The city only existed when you were driving. If you got out and walked, it was transformed into a number of endlessly scattered, vague details. The whole city experience west of the Mississippi was based on fifty miles an hour, just like the experience of Levertin's and Heidenstam's Stockholm, once upon a time, was based on the slow three miles an hour of the horse cabs (the hooves of the horses, the whir of the wheels against wet paving stones).

"The slower the vehicle, the denser the city," he said to Barbara in passing. "Consequently, the densest are the old Arabic, Greek, or Jewish cities. Because in those cities you walk, often up and down steps, very often with a laden donkey. There you achieve maximal density; it all becomes an enormous labyrinth. The different worlds we live in are all formed according to a constant, that is, man's ability to receive information during a certain period of time. And then our speed of movement varies."

"I wish I had seen a city in the old world," said Barbara. "But it seems I won't even get to California this spring either."

One of her constant ideas was to move to California. She would pack her Buick, give away her plants, sell her little house, which she had owned since 1963 when her second divorce became final, and just disappear to the west one fine morning to start a chain of stores for European and Oriental jewelry along the whole Pacific coast.

It was just that something always seemed to come up. Either she didn't have any contacts in California and couldn't see how she'd actually set up the whole thing, how she would establish herself, how she would initiate her business contacts.

Or else it was the trip itself. She often discussed routes, whether the most southerly route along the Mexican border, passing Del Rio and El Paso, then taking a slow swing to the north, would be

69

preferable, or whether it would be better to go through Colorado and then up through the Painted Desert.

In the south, you always ran the risk of meeting up with highwaymen of some kind. Nowadays you never knew; a car with out-of-state license plates was never safe, especially if it was loaded with a lot of household stuff.

Civilization in the nineteenth-century sense, in the sense which her own Jewish people had known it throughout their history, keeping it alive by persistently holding fast to their fundamental books, to their network of concepts, was now something that was simply dying out.

Taxes and universities and street lighting and safe roads, that is to say roads safe from highwaymen, were getting to be as antiquated in contemporary America as his horse cabs in Stockholm.

It was, quite simply, a different world.

"But it may be a necessary development," he said. "Perhaps it's a world that's in the process of throwing off mediocrity. I can imagine a new world, with rusting railways and disappearing factories, where the faint smoke from the philosophers' little olive-wood fires in some abandoned lot along the road will burn again.

"A world that's in the process of acquiring *concepts* once more. Texas, where people have never really been interested in making laws, where a large portion of reality has actually always been reserved for private decision-making or for the one who's got weapons—hasn't Texas, when all's said and done, slept through the industrial age? And now when the rest of the world is waking up to *inexorable reality* once more, well then, people here are better prepared than in other places.

"And in fact, isn't this unprotected and adventuresome world a good deal more honest than the huge, lying bureaucracies which squeezed their citizens dry by means of enormous tax levies and a bizarre, detailed regulation of life, but which weren't even able to give their citizens the elementary security of walking the street safely in exchange?"

"It's funny," Barbara said. "You're the quietest, most timid person I know, a typical European academic, a highbrow. But sometimes I can't help wondering if you weren't made for a quite different, much more brutal, much more adventurous life."

"Oh," he said. "It's just dreams moving in me."

It turned out to be Ingmar Bergman's *Wild Strawberries* they were to see. He had some recollection of having seen the film for the first time on an evening during Christmas break in 1957, on Kungsgatan, with a too soulful girl by the name of Monica.

Afterward you usually walked down to Stureplan.

Now they were already watching a fine old classic. The young people in the film moved through an idealized Sweden as nonexistent as his own Sweden, quiet for those who hitchhiked with the old professor, Victor Sjöström, who knew all about life on the long road along Lake Vättern which leads down to the Lund Cathedral, where the fiftieth anniversary of his doctorate will be celebrated.

It struck him how *nicely*, how precisely everyone spoke. No Peking opera could have been more stylized.

He realized that she would like to sleep with him afterward, especially since his house was on her way home. He considered this as something to be avoided. She was too persistently interested in her own orgasm, too preoccupied with silly books about female physiology and women's lib. It usually made him painfully aware of himself.

He didn't manage to avoid it.

He'd been stupid enough to borrow a book in December, just before the end of the semester, and he couldn't, at least not without being suspected of wanting to keep it, prevent her from coming in to pick it up.

Neither, of course, could he prevent her from making just a small spot of tea in his kitchen.

Nor prevent her from snuggling up to him on the couch. For some reason, she was extraordinarily good tonight. Something was singing in her, out of her fragmented, affected, half-formed, unclear soul a tune was setting itself free.

He didn't know what it was, but he felt reverence for it, perhaps also a shy, astonished gratitude, without quite knowing what he was grateful for or if he was the right person to be grateful.

"I wonder," he said thoughtfully—by then it was almost three in the morning—"I wonder if you'll ever leave for California. It seems so improbable, somehow."

"Don't be too sure," she said.

7

The lights from a car turning into the street, or perhaps turning out of it, threw reflections from the ceiling light and rotated the shadows on the ceiling.

He was alone again. He turned the pillow over, folding it in the middle in a way he'd learned as a child, when the elevator made strange sounds in the old building on Karlavägen and the shadows approached his bed. And his last thought before he went back to sleep to the familiar burr of his electronic alarm clock was a quotation:

> *Departure's dark farewell*
> *my heart already knows in secret joy.*
> *Large-eyed I gaze toward the western sky.*

In a certain sense, not readily ascertainable, he consisted of nothing but quotations. *How terribly strong this made him, he could only surmise.*

The Fugitives Discover
That They Knew Nothing

1

The negotiations were finished. He had handled his items as well as he could. He had intended to treat himself to a free day in Athens, just one, but since there was no seat on the plane, he postponed his return trip until the day before Christmas Eve.

The dark, gasoline-smelling, friendly little streets with their bizarre, Byzantine Christmas ornaments amused him. The darkness had something friendly about it. The bunches of dangling animal carcasses in the marketplace, small mustached men engaged in flowing conversations so rapid he didn't understand them, the weary youths in the cafés always engrossed in sports pages and sexual fantasies about the hair and hips of passing girls: everything calmed him. Perhaps it was the snowless streets, the mild, dry air, the smell of roast mutton. Perhaps it was the long white beards of Greek Orthodox priests or the wonderful gold mosaics displayed in the bookstore windows in expensive editions: everything calmed him.

He changed to a cheaper hotel since he was no longer on the Trade Office's expense account. This had the added advantage that his department would not be able to find him for the next few days.

He was on his way again. The turning point had been passed.

Invariably, we act first and think later. Even world history only acquires meaning in retrospect. Authors create their models by allowing themselves to be inspired by them, thus making them visible. Children invent their parents by allowing themselves to be influenced by them, and, when they need excuses for failure and decline, even to be deformed by them.

It's rare for someone who has just bought a car to start familiarizing himself with its characteristics and technical performance right away. In fact, knowledge comes later in order to justify the decision, to confer meaning on it.

This means that life takes on a circular shape: we act in order to justify the acts which we have already committed. We take steps whose only function is to give meaning to the steps we have already taken.

Obstinately, we stay on at the bad hotel in order to give meaning to the fact that we were once stupid enough to check in there.

Historians seem to have problems understanding why the poor laborers along the Swedish Norrland coast beat up the first socialist agitators who approached them.

That isn't very difficult to understand: if the agitators were right, then these people had suffered and worked meaninglessly for the most part, and that, of course, is a thought which is easier to attack with a fist in the face than it is to accept.

In actual fact we hate everything that wants to tell us that we are not at the center.

On one of the small streets next to Athen's Syntagma Place, with its elegant cafés and Hotel Angelterre like an aristocratic old lady presiding over it all, the American bar has been located for several decades.

It wasn't hard to find it again. He went in mostly because a chilly evening wind, a real December wind, blowing in from the Saronic Gulf started to make it unpleasant out in the street. He had been there many times before. The thought of American apple turnovers awoke a kind of perverse enthusiasm in him.

As soon as he walked in, he saw Linda. She must have been close to forty now. Her beautiful black hair had gotten a few gray strands, that was all. The same large, almond-shaped Southern eyes, the same boyish head, the same habit of nervously twisting a pearl necklace in her left hand, kind of pulling it over her left breast.

74

She was a capable international economist, married to a quiet novelist in Rochester.

The last time he'd seen her was a beautiful summer day in New England, in 1973. He had given her and two of her boys a ride to an outdoor pool, and on the way they had talked quite a bit about the offside rule in European soccer, which at that time was something rather new and elite in America.

He had liked her a lot then.

She was just as beautiful on this December evening. A little more loquacious, a little livelier, perhaps a touch more nervous than he remembered her. She wore a long brown dress, matching brown shoes, a brown sweater with a turned-up wool collar which accentuated her long neck.

Over her shoulders, she wore a jacket of rather coarse fur.

She had been at a conference with the Organization for Economic Co-operation and Development. Lots of their mutual acquaintances from American universities and European expert committees had been there. What a pity he hadn't known. She herself was about to leave, not for home, but going in the opposite direction, so to speak, to the December-dark Aegean.

A woman friend, a painter from Utica, N.Y., had bought a house on Hydra, one of the nearby islands in the small archipelago closest to Athens, in what's called the Saronic Gulf.

This was a very wise friend, of course. Now, after the collapse of Beirut as a central point for the economy and the transfer of capital in the Mediterranean area, when the role of Beirut had started to be taken over by Athens, real-estate prices on the nearby islands were bound to rise phenomenally. Nobody could stand a city like Athens in the long run.

Wasn't it peculiar, by the way, that nowadays the line between rich and poor countries went between those which could afford emission control and unleaded gasoline and those which, like Yugoslavia and Greece, kept using malodorous and dangerous leaded gasoline?

Her friend was probably no great painter, she was divorced too,

75

and she lived mostly in the Saronic Gulf in the winter. But now her mother in Boston was on her deathbed, and she was spending the winter there. Her name was Leonora.

"Linda," he said, suddenly, and not without enthusiasm remembering her name, "your husband isn't along this time."

"It's a bit complicated," she said. "It's been very complicated for a while. Leonora needed a housesitter—you know, in California they talk about housesitting the way you used to talk about babysitting. And I needed to get away for a while.

"Let's talk about something else."

Wasn't Christmas *always* a problem for *everyone*? He himself had been divorced seven years now, he didn't really like it, but at least it had one advantage: you didn't have to make a thing about Christmas, didn't have to pretend to be in a mental state different from the one you were actually in.

That *was* an advantage.

He asked if he could buy her a bourbon. It turned out there was bourbon. Someone in the group started talking about the American women's movement. Not so different from Ibsen's *A Doll's House*, actually. Except now they had credit cards. A modern Nora would have had a credit card and wouldn't have had to resort to a sleazy lawyer to get a personal loan. Then they talked about the American dollar and the American credit economy and the risk of the whole system collapsing one fine day.

And strangely enough, they were back to the women's movement.

"If I were a woman, I'd be a lesbian," he said. "Profoundly lesbian. Doing it with men: unspeakably disgusting. Men are hairy, and you don't have to have visited the locker room of a tennis club to realize how bad men smell."

She agreed completely. Lesbian love was the only esthetically acceptable love.

He asked if she were on her way somewhere, if he could take her some place.

It turned out that she was taking an early boat to her island the next morning. Because it was the morning before Christmas Eve, and on Christmas Eve all the boats would probably be full of Greeks.

Where was she staying?

At the Athens Hilton.

Not bad.

Yes, but there weren't very many hotels to choose from at Christmas.

What was that red book he'd put on the bar?

It was Ephraem Syrus of Nisibis, a fourth-century Syrian poet. He had written hymns of paradise, great, blue-eyed, all-encompassing paradise hymns, intended for a Christianity as yet uncontaminated by the Greeks, free of Plato and Aristotle.

Ephraem had lived at a time of uninterrupted military occupations, sieges, razed monasteries, hanged monks. And a Christian church surrounded by enemies for the past century: Jews, Arians, Manicheans, Marcionites, Gnostics, and supporters of Zarathustra.

What did it say in his paradise hymns?

That in paradise there would be an unlimited supply of butter.

What was so unreasonable about that?

She had met an interesting Indian dancer, male, yes, who had told her about conditions in Calcutta and Bombay.

Of course, ignorant people, experts on the Third World, might imagine that there was something particularly *Indian* about starving people.

What they were actually seeing was a normal state of affairs, already described by Malthus. Ths slums of Paris and London in the beginning of the nineteenth century, described by historical witnesses, looked just the same as Calcutta and Bombay. In the early 1840s, in Paris, people slept or dozed on the sidewalks in order to save energy just as much as they do in Calcutta.

Texas, Switzerland, the Federal Republic of Germany—they are nothing but shiny bubbles on the surface of events. The elementary thing is poverty, the fundamental conditions are and will be Malthus' and Darwin's.

He was a cynic?

A cynic from having sat on too many committees of the United Nations' relief organizations?

Perhaps he was a cynic. He had to point out to her that he hadn't made society's laws.

It was a great thing in an evil world to have written a book, like Ephraem Syrus of Nisibis. The people in the big, shiny bubbles of temporary overconsumption were too spoiled to realize it. That is why those books written outside the bubbles, outside of Rome, outside of Byzantium, outside of Harvard, were important to read in a way. They had higher *specific gravity*. And he translated for her directly from the bizarre New Testament Greek:

> *When, in his daring,*
> *Adam ran to eat thereof,*
> *for a moment the two kinds of knowledge*
> *descended over him,*
> *turning the two veils aside,*
> *that had once obscured his sight,*
> *He saw the holiness of the Holy Ones, saw their splendor;*
> *He trembled;*
> *He saw his presumption:*
> *He was confused, trembled, grieved,*
> *For the two insights he had won*
> *were to him a wretchedness.*

He'd always been a fantastic linguist. She had heard that from her first husband, who had worked with him in Jordan in the '60s.

Had he become pious, too?

What did she mean by pious?

If, for instance, people in the U.S. started living in accordance with the torrent of pious admonition emanating from their TV sets every Sunday morning, not unlike Niagara Falls, if they started living by the ethics of altruism which their clergy preached on Sunday mornings, instead of by the ethics of maximum gain which they ordinarily followed, society would probably go under in less than a week.

No, what the hell did she mean? Couldn't you be interested in an early Christian poet without being suspected of being some kind of Baptist? Look at these Greeks, for instance. Damn it all, there wasn't even one little rock in their sea where there wasn't a chapel, a saint's image, a small white church, not a mountaintop that was not the refuge of some bearded monks, living like sand martins in some monastery, barely clinging to the outcroppings of their rock. Were there any people, except possibly Turks, who were worse than Greeks at exploiting the misfortunes of others to make money? Was there another country in the world where it was the practice for steamers to leave ahead of schedule just to be able to charge extra to go back and take on passengers?

"Of course," he replied. Had she ever had a traffic accident in Mexico? If you had a traffic accident in Mexico and still had a car that worked, there was only one thing to do: get the hell out of there, but fast. In countries where deep piety exists, there was also ruthless greed. In his experience, only wealth could create a bit of compassion and tolerance in the world, albeit temporarily. The poor couldn't afford it. This did not prevent Ephraem Syrus from being a very worthwhile poet.

What did she want, anyway? If he remembered correctly, there used to be dancing on the top floor of the Athens Hilton, a bar and a dance orchestra. They danced and had some difficulty finding space on the dance floor, since some cruise ship had evidently landed an enormous bunch of middle-aged Americans, dressed in vineleaf wreaths which suggested aging Priapuses or honorary doctors at a Swedish university.

He liked dancing with her. She developed a mild, ruttish glow which kept increasing. She had an obvious sense of rhythm—this was a musical woman. She danced very well, in fact.

Sometimes they were at least ten feet apart. By and by, she came closer.

A bit girlishly, she shivered when he put his thigh between her legs.

What did she want? Was the way to orgasm long or short for her?

Did she like having her breasts touched?

No, they weren't particularly small.

79

He liked small breasts.

On the whole, he liked boyish women. This was probably due to suppressed homosexual tendencies.

On the whole, he liked ambiguity.

Did she like him to suck her there?

She hadn't quite got there yet.

In the moonlight streaming in generously through the big picture window, she looked not unlike a small, crouching frog. He left her for a moment so he could look at her.

He had a lot of self-confidence.

As soon as life started looking like reality, it always seemed so grotesque, so bizarre.

After that he got her easily. Like many women, she had a kind of agreeable dryness just before her orgasm.

They left quite early the next morning, and it wasn't easy to get a cab. The road to the Piraeus harbor is one of the ugliest, most dreary in the world, and the only amusing thing was the overelaborate, somewhat Byzantine Christmas decorations hanging across the dirty, monotonous streets, where they repeatedly got stuck in traffic while motorbikes that seemed to have been assembled in the kitchens of their owners passed the lines of cars in clouds of blue, leaded smoke.

Along the road, huge stands selling ballpoint pens, small transistors, and cigarette lighters showed that the world of high technology had found the poor in this district.

2

It turned out not to be hydrofoils this time, those "Flying Dolphins" that they both knew from several convention excursions.

It was an ordinary, tall, white coastal steamer. He paid the cab, brought their luggage on board, bought first-class tickets, and was just thinking of making reservations for lunch when he discovered that she was gone.

At the risk of their luggage being stolen, he searched the boat deck by deck, even standing steadfastly outside some ladies' rooms.

She simply wasn't there, and that was that.

He took out Ephraem and sat down on the foredeck. The sun was warm, although it was the day before Christmas Eve.

A gentle breeze blew straight into the Gulf of Piraeus. They would be on board for at least four hours.

He found her in third class, talking to a Greek family consisting of a strawberry-blonde painter—when Greek women are blonde, they are always strawberry blonde in a wonderful, intensely pictorial manner which makes you think of long-vanished Mediterranean cultures—her husband, a quiet bald gentleman, immersed in his morning paper, and children of different ages who all seemed to have brought along a variety of pets, from guinea pigs to canaries.

In the midst of this family circle going to the island of Hydra, she seemed to enjoy herself.

Since she did not give the least sign of knowing she had been missed, he didn't let on that he had missed her.

Kyria Tulla was a well-known painter in Athens. She was going to Hydra with her husband, going to a house she had owned there since the '60s. She spoke of the island for at least an hour, while the boat steamed further and further into the watery labyrinth of the Saronic Gulf.

The Peloponnesus was already standing on the right-hand horizon like a dark shadow. Over it hovered winter clouds, heavy with rain. That's the way it generally was.

Winter stayed inside, over the Peloponnesus.

In summer, the island was usually inundated with rich foreign tourists. A wealthy international crowd thronged the little bars around the harbor; there was a certain tendency among those waterfront bars to become gathering places for American homosexuals. The local inhabitants were squeezed into the higher parts of the town, which was shaped like an amphitheater.

It didn't matter that much.

The higher parts were so much cooler and better.

She knew Linda's friend, the painter from Utica, very well. Oh yes, she had been painting like the American Abstract Expressionists for a long time now, about like Pollock, an extremely Expressionist kind of painting.

Nowadays, she seemed to have taken a ninety-degree turn: landscapes reminiscent of the American Neo-Gothic, almost Romantic actually, something of Caspar David Friedrich.

That house was very high up; it was a nice house because it had two terraces with a view of the whole harbor.

Before the American painter had bought it—it was early in the '60s, before the run on houses on Greek islands had started in earnest—it had belonged to a lady who was also called Leonora, strangely enough.

There had been rumors on the island that this Leonora was a witch. It was hard to say whether she actually was one: her house, like most genuine Hydra houses, had a large underground water-storage tank (it was thanks to those underground water tanks that the Turks had never obtained any real power on the island), and in the '20s at least, in the days of Kyria's mother, there had been rumors of strange, frightening noises coming from the water tank in the house at night.

At twilight, the wind freshened; it was a red, dramatic twilight which descended early. To the north were banked clouds, clouds that were rain and which, still further north, must be the first big December storm, blizzards coming to establish the reign of winter in northern Europe.

Just after dusk they passed through the last bay, rounded a headland, and suddenly there was Hydra's harbor in front of them, opening like a veritable pirate harbor, protected by a fort with ancient cannon. The harbor seemed momentarily too small for the boat. When at last it had been moored properly, the bow leaned forward toward one of the lampposts in the harbor, conveying the bizarre impression of a boat about to founder on a lamppost.

There was not a single soul in sight. The water was at least two inches about the harbor pavement. His socks and shoes wet, he managed to get into a grocery store where yellow lightbulbs threw a faint circle of light.

Inside was the smell of sawdust, oil, salted olives, and strong detergents perpetually associated with Greek grocery stores.

Soon Kyra Tulla's whole family was in the store. This got the chatting Greeks moving; they hadn't paid the least attention to him.

Just like in Sweden, he thought. A milieu where everything depends on having the right connections and where nobody exists until he has shown that such a network of connections surrounds him.

The water in the harbor seemed to be rising, the wind picked up; people squeezed together in the grocery store.

During this time, he did not speak to her.

She took the opportunity of buying some loaves of bread: wonderful, large, fragrant loaves of bread, and a bottle of local wine, a couple of smoked sausages. Darkness pressed close outside.

The Athenian painter got her donkeys first, but she made very sure that there was another donkey for what she called her "American friends."

The man with the donkey was not particularly talkative. He refused to take the foreigners' Greek seriously and answered their grammatically correct, well-formulated sentences in a kind of baby talk intended for tourists: "Very much wind, yes, much water, very cold autumn, yes. Cold yes."

He was momentarily tempted to answer, "Very little Greek, yes, very little syntax, yes? Very small head?"

But he refrained, since he suddenly realized that his aggressiveness was much too great to have been caused by that man with the donkey.

The man got his money. He coaxed the door open. By now she was very small, very tired; she had wrapped a black wool shawl over her head.

Through the dark streets, they heard only the sound of the wind and the sound of the donkey on its way back down the steps.

And between the gusts of wind something that must have been the sound of sheep bells, sheep grazing on the fresh, green December grass.

No way was he able to get the electric light turned on.

Groping about on innumerable landings, up and down steps that took him by surprise, always holding an anxiously fluttering wax candle which the wind threatened to extinguish every time he passed through one of the courtyards. (He didn't know for sure whether it was the same courtyard or more than one, but he had time to notice a pile of heavy, solid wood, perhaps oak or olive wood—he wondered where the ax might be and how he would be able to start a fire.)

He found the fuses, the Mediterranean type, which you start up by pressing a small button (in the Mediterranean area, you don't like to throw things away, and the producers of electricity had long since realized this and acted accordingly), but no matter how long he pressed, it didn't do any good.

The electricity in the house must be turned off.

But the water was running. He heard a flush somewhere on the second floor.

He went back into the central courtyard and fetched a good-sized bundle of wood. The wind was rising.

It wasn't as hard to get the dense wood, with its rock-hard, black surface, to catch as you'd have thought. He found methanol in the kitchen, old newspapers in a cupboard beside the dark, empty refrigerator with its faint smell of scouring powder.

It struck him that it would be fun to know what the rooms and the walls looked like in this house. The feeble flame of the tallow, or rather wax, candle could only tell him *that* there were paintings on the walls, figurative ones, perhaps some kind of depictions of saints: there was nothing more he could find out.

"*The whole damn Western culture is a house like this,*" he said when he found her again at last and had made her sit down on the old, shaggy, very friendly sheepskin rug in front of the fireplace.

The wind was still gaining in force. He contemplated going up on the upper-level balcony to see whether there were whitecaps out there, whether there was a full moon. The olive trees on the slope above them seemed to groan in the movements of the wind. By this time, the passages and ventilation shafts in the house were whining and whistling to such a degree that a horrid voice from the closed water cistern could not have made itself heard among all the other voices.

"This is the only warm spot," he said. "Let's sleep here tonight, in front of the fire. *Then the cold will wake us up as soon as the fire is about to go out,* and then we'll put more wood on."

Sleep overpowered them with surprising speed.

3

When he woke up, the storm had not abated—on the contrary, it seemed like the whole house was a giant pipe it was blowing on. The shutters banged, muffled sounds emanated from the chimney flues, as from a giant flute, an olive tree knocked against a window with hard knuckles.

White arches and deep window embrasures emerged in the diffuse light of dawn. An object he'd repeatedly stumbled over the night before turned out to be a stool of solid oak. In a corner of the room stood an easel.

She had fallen asleep in front of the fire under a pile of blankets. Now he couldn't see her any more, but since he'd already gotten used to her disappearances, it didn't bother him as much.

A strange Christmas Eve morning, he thought. Today there will be no boats to Piraeus.

He found her upstairs. She was sitting there quietly, crying.

He did not ask her why.

Electric bills were paid at City Hall. The sum asked for the six months when the house had been standing empty for the winter— the lady in Boston couldn't very well have used up much electricity—corresponded to the electric bill a small car repair shop would have run up in half a year in Sweden. He went from room to room in the little City Hall, where, strangely enough, all the employees seemed to be working even though it was Christmas Eve. He saw women waiting humbly, wrapped in black veils, and fishermen with big, red, experienced hands, and the office employees: small, twisted, ratlike.

He thought of Sartre's words, "But can't you see that they are all villains?"

With a kind of weariness which had become more and more familiar to him over the years, he went to the mayor, complained loudly about the bill before anyone had time to stop him, and forgot an envelope containing half the sum on the mayor's desk.

He knew that when he returned to the house, the electricity would be on. The water was high in the harbor; there was not a single boat there, and the sea ran black outside the breakwater.

In a corner of the pier, there was still some wood, black, oddly twisted pieces of olive wood from the woods up on the Peleponnesus. He bought two donkeyloads, bought bread, looked at a five-day-old copy of an Athens newspaper at the tobacconist's—it seemed that serious problems were in the offing for the Shah of Iran, any idiot could tell you that, and he returned to the house around eleven.

She was sitting by the light of a candle, dressed in a dark veil, no, in a dark, probably very expensive wool shawl which she had wrapped over her head, playing old saints' hymns on an ivory flute that she must have found in one of the boxes in the house.

"What are you playing?" he asked.

"*Hymnus Unius Sanctis,*" she said.

She was getting a cold.

Around three in the afternoon, a kindly old American who owned a house three doors down in the same lane dropped in. He was an old friend of the lady from Boston and wanted to see what kind of people were staying there. His mother lived in Memphis, Tennessee, and he wondered how long he could let her be on her own. She was almost eighty, and he himself was past sixty. He had lived here since the '50s. But he missed his wife terribly. She had died in 1961. They had discovered the island together, soon after the war.

It had been a great adventure when they'd settled here at last.

And the island would never be the same again, now that she was gone.

Two hours later, he brought over some copies of *Time* magazine, in case they hadn't read them.

He told them there was a restaurant on the island that was open this time of year and which might be worth a visit. But it probably wouldn't be open on Christmas Eve.

In the evening, after a dinner that was simple considering it was Christmas Eve—anchovies, olives, retsina, fresh bread—they tried playing Pretorius as a duet. He had found a box full of dusty old recorders. Some hung together and others had dried apart.

"I could easily love you," he said. "Your round little shoulders, your liveliness, your laughter. You still have something enigmatic for me."

Why do we need the enigmatic in people in order to love them?

"You, too, have something enigmatic left," she said.

The wind was starting to subside.

"Nonsense." And he didn't quite know why he spoke that way.

The day after Christmas, the first boat arrived, with more foreigners, more property owners who wanted to visit their houses, a new shipment of American canned goods, and a group from the U.S. teeming around the harbor without the travelers actually knowing what they were doing.

They brought the friendly American to the restaurant, which was open. It was trying ambitiously to be French, with frogs legs and a house pâté and omelets.

They were the first guests.

Then they seemed to arrive from every direction all at once.

"That's Lynda," the American said. Lynda was a ruddy, rather heavy-set, perhaps maternal girl with reddish hair. Or actually she was no longer a girl. She had two children along, around seven or eight, and two men, lean, coquettish, a bit red in the face.

"One of them is Lynda's husband," said the American. "He's a very famous painter. He often exhibits in New York and Paris. And the other one is some kind of friend of his."

The two men seemed to ignore the woman called Lynda completely. The American said hello to her when she looked toward their table. All three of them said hello. She seemed to have very tired, very wise eyes.

"The things women put up with," he said.

"What do you mean," she said.

"Homosexual men, indifference, the brutal whims of others, everything—everything, if only you give the impression that you want something with them."

"I don't know what you mean," she said.

The American kept silent; he was much preoccupied with a steak *au poivre.*

Quickly a coldness spread between them.

I must have said something totally wrong, he thought.

On the way back it rained, a fine, ubiquitous drizzle. It settled on his glasses and made it hard to see. The lanes they walked through were so narrow that they had to stop here and there to let people walk by them in the opposite direction.

They said goodbye to the American in front of his house. For some reason, he seemed quite relieved. The wind had now died down completely.

Their own window shone inviting and yellow; the electricity was back on. They entered and shook the water from their clothes.

She had on her beautiful shawl. It was reddish brown, heavy, hanging over one shoulder. It was dripping wet.

"Let's have a drink," he said. "We'll have a drink in the kitchen."

As a matter of fact, they'd already had too many.

There was a kind of counter in the kitchen, a bar counter actually. It separated the kitchen from the big, studiolike living room. On it stood a row of bottles. Some of them had to have been ancient.

He found a Scotch whiskey, Old Parr, which he'd never heard of.

His shoes were still wet; he should take his shoes and socks off as soon as possible.

This damn civilization really *is* done for, he thought.

In my youth, there was still some hope; we walked through flowering orchards on our way home from dances in Uppsala in May, and we imagined that there must be some kind of future within the conditions of this world, something we would be able to accomplish.

She was sitting at the table, small and alone. She had another shawl over her head.

It gave her shadow a magnified, grotesque appearance.

Right now she wasn't looking at him. Thoughtfully, he lifted the bottle, weighing it in his hand. It would be so easy to throw it.

"You're a vampire," he said. "Not literally, of course, but psychologically. You're living on the blood of other people, borrowing their experiences, their vitality."

"Just imagine," she said, looking up at him with a very pale face, "I've been sitting here thinking the same thing about you. You're living on others. If there were no others, you'd dissolve and fly away like a moth, like some of the other creatures that fly in the night."

"I'm leaving tomorrow," he said.

The next morning, there was a new storm. No boats. An irate Australian had been at the beach café waiting for boats since eight o'clock.

"Those damn Greeks are good-for-nothings," he said. "Their talk of seafaring traditions is just ridiculous. In this weather, people go out fishing in small boats in Australia. The Greeks piss in their pants they're that scared if it's more than three on the Beaufort scale."

"I'm sorry about what happened last night," he said. "But that girl Lynda with her two men set off something awful in me, a kind of horror, terror, rage, I don't know what."

"I know," she said. "Take it easy now. You might help me do something about the upstairs toilet instead, it keeps running."

They didn't speak much to each other the two days that the storm lasted. Paradoxically, they slept together at night, and these nightly sex acts were stormier than the weather outside.

On the afternoon of the third day, the storm ended. The heavy carpet of clouds moved, like a curtain, eighty miles to the west and settled in its usual spot, above the Peloponnesus.

The winters can't have been much different in the days of Ephraem, he thought. Down in the harbor, people started assembling by the pier.

She accompanied him all the way down. During the course of this walk, he realized that he loved her. It was a very great relief when the boat came.

She made a small sign from the pier, a sign, or the hesitant attempt at a sign, which was supposed to mean, "Write to me," or, "I'll write to you."

Later they exchanged a few very polite letters, conscious that they had come close to something great, and that they would never be able to mention it to anyone.

Greatness arrived. And they were unable to receive it.

Greatness Strikes Where It Pleases

He came from one of the small farms up by the woods; strange things come from there now and then.

Tumbledown barns in the meadows, sometimes with the ridge of the roof broken right in the middle, small cow barns made from cinderblock, unusable after the milk trucks got too wide for the small roads.

And the road into the woods: like a green tunnel. When he was a boy, he played between the barn and the house and was always forbidden to go behind the barn into the woods.

The woods were marshy, with all kinds of mushrooms and toadstools, a place rich in different species the way it sometimes happens where the shadows linger a long time and different kinds of rock mingle.

It was quite a small place; his brother and sister were both older, by two and three years.

His first school was the woodshed; his brother and sister were often there, whittling boats and cars out of wood. They were practising their way into tools. He himself had a horror of them, perhaps due to some unsuccessful early attempts, a horror of the sharp edges of the chisels that could cut into your nail like a knife into butter, the axes and the big timber cleavers with their worn handles, and, worst of all, the saws hanging in a long row on their nails, from the big two-handed lumberman's saws with their bows and clasps to the crosscut saws, the joiner's saws with their buckle pegs that clattered so merrily when you released the tension, the one-man crosscut saws that, oddly enough, were called "tails" although they had nothing to do with tails—grownups had such funny names for their things: that was their peculiarity, and they had a *right* to all those names which he didn't have. He always laughed awkwardly and crept into a corner when his brother and sister tried to teach him those names.

Those things belonged to them: dovetail saws, punches. The old wooden mallet used for pounding in fence posts, made from curly birch, battered by tens of thousands of strikes of wood against wood, impossible to lift.

And above them all, hanging majestically: the ice saw, absolutely forbidden to touch, a cruel giant with dragon's teeth, a magnification of the other saws, crueller than they, but also silent, waiting, never used.

He would dream of the teeth of all the saws.

Sometimes they hit him, but not very badly. Anyway, they hit him when he came from the woodshed with wounds and gashes from the tools in the woodshed. They were afraid that he'd really hurt himself. They wanted to keep him away from the tools.

His brother and sister, who knew how, were allowed to handle them. It gave him the feeling that the words, too, belonged to them.

Sometimes they might send him to fetch tools that did not exist, "bench marks," things like that.

It gave him a feeling that it would always be vague and uncertain which things existed in the world and which did not. Evidently using words was harder than you might imagine.

They always laughed loudly, doubled up with laughter when he returned empty-handed, or when they had fooled him into going to the far end of the barn searching for impossible objects.

In actual fact, the strong decided what words should be used for.

Mushrooms were better. They didn't care about having names. They had smells instead, strong, earthy smells, smells of decaying leaves, of heated iron, of oxidizing copper, some of them like rotting animals and some with mysterious smells that didn't exist anywhere else.

And their shapes: most of them round, but all of them round in different ways. Some had a depression in the middle, as if the whole thing had been rotated around the midpoint at enormous speed, just once, then solidifying; some had indentations, wavy shapes; some had tall, narrow stems; some had a collar; some, delicate gills under the cap, so fragile that they crumbled at the slightest touch. And there were some with organworks of fine pipes.

Sometimes they were covered with slime that made you pull your hand back quickly. Sometimes they were dry, brown, friendly to your fingers, as if they'd pulled the sunshine into themselves and still preserved this sunshine like a secret force under the skin.

And then those strange things that came up late in the fall, smelling like mushrooms but still not looking like mushrooms but like something else: a red finger groping its way between two rocks, a strangely solid pat of butter forgotten on a cranberry leaf, something indescribably gray fermenting, growing, turning in the fissures of a rotting treetrunk.

He felt a kinship, a friendship between himself and these cool objects without names that changed day by day and which always disappeared again like formless clumps of decomposing life in the moss.

He minded the ban on going to the mushrooms more than the ban on going to the tools.

The fall when he turned seven and was going to start school turned into a disaster.

It was a small school, down by the lake, a one-room school with a single teacher, a small, broad man with gold-rimmed glasses and strong, blunt hands.

Decades later, he could still remember the teacher's broad, strong fingernails with a kind of approval. They looked like those objects that really exist.

He was going to learn to read, and the teacher was both kind and helpful. He sat for a long time on a chair beside him, smelling of strange smells, tobacco and Palmolive soap.

The letters were easy to tell apart, but he never got any words out of them. They didn't want to speak.

That wasn't anything to wonder at. He didn't have any words to counter them with, nothing to meet them with. Nothing at all. He tried copying them, and they turned into mushrooms.

It seemed natural that he should walk around by himself during recess, digging with a stick in the gravel, while his brother and sister played with their friends.

There was nothing that wasn't completely self-evident, and he simply couldn't understand what he was doing in school. It was noisy. It bothered him to hear too many children laughing and shouting to each other at the same time.

He was homesick, and when it got to be afternoon, a wind came through the big ash trees outside the schoolhouse.

The trees are so happy, he thought, when the wind comes. That gives them something to do.

Actually he only went to school for a week.

What he could remember of it afterward was that it was where he first smelled a smell that would later become very familiar to him: the smell of scouring powder and disinfectant, the smell of hospitals, the smell in the waiting room at the county doctor's, strong in some places and weaker in others, but always the same, varying in one way or the other: *the smell of those who wanted something from him.*

The lunch music and the voices on the radio. The voices on the radio became important to him later on; they affirmed his continued existence, they hovered around him, especially at dinner time, cheery, sometimes persuasive, voices that filled the air, music that filled the air and didn't want anything from him.

That was later. After they'd come to get him.

They came and got him one afternoon that fall. His parents evidently were expecting it, his mother in her good dress and with a cardboard suitcase tied with a piece of string (he would encounter it again and again for a couple of decades; at last it became identified with his mother); wartime taxi with a producer-gas unit

94

rumbling dully in the rear, roads and carsick vomiting on the way to the city.

Then the House, large, white, behind trees and a fence. And the smell of those who wanted something from him.

All new smells. The aides, in their dresses with high collars and maternal aprons—they were often older women, round and sturdy—had a different smell. The food smelled different, was different, starchy, gravyish, floating, wetter than at home in the woods. It was eaten in a common dining room during terrible rattling and spilling. Some of his new schoolmates had a hard time managing their spoons. Some of them let the food run out of the corners of their mouths.

He was afraid of them.

They didn't do anything to him. Most of them moved slowly; some were so deep in their own worlds that nothing could have disturbed them.

They were all so far beyond language, the language of the others, the foreign languages, that there was nothing for them to quarrel about.

They shared the same living space, and there was enough food for everybody.

The food was important: it was like a maternal outflowing, a welcoming smell, a connection to the other world which was not a prohibition.

That took time to discover.

The first fall he was too paralysed to feel such things. He still missed his own world, the woodshed, his mushrooms, the smell of milk strained in the barn while it was still warm; the funny, wet snouts of the pigs, the laces high up on his father's boots, always muddy, swinging rhythmically around the bootlegs when he went out in the morning.

He missed a world.

He found a spider under his bed that he used to play with silently in the evening, until he happened to pick it apart, leg by leg.

He was too interested in seeing how it was made.

The boy in the bed next to him was shapelessly fat, wet his bed regularly, and cried in his sleep. When he had the chance, he made little paper balls and ate them. He could tear them out of a magazine someone had forgotten in the dayroom, or tear strips from a bag left behind on a table in the large, dark hall. He tore at the wallpaper by the door until someone told him he wasn't allowed to do that.

Sometimes he'd feed the boy paper. It was fun to see how fast it disappeared.

The boy in the bed on the other side of him wasn't much fun. He was silent.

But the wallpaper, especially in the morning, with its faded blue and pink lines, the wallpaper was almost the first thing that comforted him. The lines crossed and veered apart again; they made shapes. You could make trees, big, intricate trees with limbs that branched off and then branched off again, all the way up to the ceiling.

You could let one tree copy another, so that there were two mirror trees opposite one another on each wall, one in the shade and the other in the sun.

He could lie like that for such a long time, building trees, that they thought he was sick in the morning.

He was just making a tree that was reflecting itself inside itself when the aide came and made him get up. She looked curiously at his sheets.

He belonged to those who washed themselves. He had a habit of sucking the celluloid handle of his toothbrush for a long time.

The knots in his shoelaces were the worst. The knot was a small, evil animal that the lace passed through. The lace and the knot weren't the same thing, for you could make the same knot with different kinds of lace.

His knots were always terribly complicated.

Spring came, and suddenly, in the space of one day, they were all sent home. It was April 1940, and the House was going to be used for something else.

His mother came. She praised him and said he'd grown.

She had coffee with the aides, and it sounded as if they were talking in pretend voices.

At home, the snow was melting. His brother and sister had grown a lot more than he had, and the old horse had died and was buried by the pasture.

He'd never liked it. It had large, yellow, menacing teeth, and it had a way of tossing its head around in the half-light of the barn that scared him.

It was gone, and that was as it should be.

After he'd been home a week, he almost drowned in a brook when he went too far out on the crumbling edge of the ice close to a waterfall. He got a good hiding.

It was his brother who pulled him out. One of his red boots stuck in the mud. His brother poked around for it with a fence pole for quite some time, while the boy stood there shivering. He cried, for he knew that the worst was yet to come.

The water still stung in his nose; water you inhale deeply has a strange way of stinging.

The first coltsfoot was growing beside his own foot, which was heavy with mud. His nose was running, he shook with cold, his thin overalls smelled damp and putrid from the brook water. He stood quite still, freezing, and someone somewhere owed him infinite love.

Not a trace of mushrooms in April.

The spring of 1945, just when World War II was ending, he learned to masturbate.

He thought he had made a fantastic discovery: he could surprise himself.

He rubbed the thing which grew more and more like a mushroom, preferably against the right side of his bed, and pondered his wallpaper trees, went deeper and deeper into them, and had done it many times with increasing desire, with excitement, a feeling that the world was becoming *denser* that way, the first time he discovered that there was an ending. The first time it scared

97

him: his body knew something he didn't know it knew. It could do something he'd never believed it could do.

How many such secrets did it hold? How many new, secret pockets could it open?

And was he the only one in the world who could do it? In a way, it was the happiest spring of his life.

They made it clear to him that he was doing something forbidden, especially the older aides, who had a way of being *disgusted* by it. But they weren't too severe. It was to be expected.

Now he had himself for a playmate, for a mirror. He was no longer alone. He started to grow and got quite tall. Mirror and reflection grew together and couldn't be separated. And still they had their secret conversations. The trees in the wallpaper acquired depth.

At this time, between 1945 and 1950 approximately, he was very close to something that might have been an awakening.

He was moved to another room—without wallpaper—and stood in the door of the wood shop, following with an interested gaze those who could carve.

A new teacher came, a lean, rather tall young man with gentle brown eyes who allowed him to straighten up, to sort pieces of wood in the lumber room from the very beginning; who didn't let on when the older students laughed at him.

He was not allowed close to the saws and the chisels, but he was allowed to use the sandpaper and to help hold the glue clamps when they were put around pieces of wood on which the glue was still bubbling from the heat in the pot.

The new teacher—he never knew his name—was almost as silent as he was himself. He moved with calm, determined steps between the tool cabinets and the benches, kept the paint cans and the lumber in order. He always looked him in the eye when he gave him something to do, a board to carry, a floor to sweep. He looked him in the eye and let it be known that he actually existed. When he handed him a pail of wood shavings to empty, it became a living sign saying that he existed.

The students in this workshop were of different kinds and different ages. Some things happened that frightened him a bit

98

and that amused him almost as much. Clumsy as calves, older and younger boys moved around each other, joked, butted each other. Jokes and taunts occurred, glue pots in the hair and boards nailed to the floor when you went to pick them up.

It disturbed him and frightened him when it was directed against him. The laughter was something they tried to force on him.

The board in the floor was a surprise directed at someone they wanted him to be. Something to laugh at. But that wasn't where he was.

The new teacher knew how to quiet such things down; with a calm hand, without harsh words, he separated the combatants when the boys got into a fight, dragging each other around a bench, keeping a strong hold on each other's hair. Patiently, he showed that you can't plane a board from both directions without ripping up the fibers. He never allowed dirt to accumulate under his short, broad nails.

He was, in a way, the center of the world.

In a world that had no center, he reigned like a quiet monarch, too self-evident ever to feel that his own order was being threatened, too rich to demand anything from the poor, an envoy in chaos serving an order so noble that it was also able to accept the necessity of disorder.

There were those who urinated in the pails of wood shavings because they didn't have time to get to the toilets inside the main entrance.

They had to clean it up themselves, but no harsh words were spoken.

It was somewhat different with the women aides. They were so divided between disgust and maternity, or locked into a maternity which was disgust at the same time, that they always created anxiety.

They smelled different. Their large, white forearms, often a bit reddened, fascinated him, and he often tried to touch them, but they nudged him gently aside. He was "in the way," as they called it.

He suspected great secrets in them, sniffed out that he was only seeing a narrow strip of their lives, but he wasn't able to formulate it.

They changed often, so that there was no possibility of keeping a face in your memory: as the years passed, their faces merged into a single face, and it was gentle and mute.

He himself slipped away, too. The wood shop teacher moved after a couple of years; the shop was closed, since the students who had worked there moved to another kind of institution. Quite a few disappeared, and only the hopeless ones remained.

The traffic along the road increased during those years. In the spring of 1952, a trailer truck loaded with grain lost control swerving to avoid a youth on a Husqvarna 125 cc; the trailer went through the loose sand on the shoulder of the road, and the whole thing turned over in their hedge.

The driver climbed out, a bit shaken up, and saw two hydrocephalic boys tumbling like little seals in the yellow grain that filled the ditch.

He thought he'd landed in another world.

The salvage went quickly, but they scooped up wheat for weeks down in the ditch, played with it, filled their pockets with it. The aides found wheat under the beds, in the pillow cases, everywhere.

It was a mysterious gift, and it came from outside.

It was the last big event for a long time. His senses were asleep: there was nothing that made enough of a claim on them. He lived for mealtimes, and when he was around thirty, he became grotesquely fat. His blue carpenter's pants with suspender buckles had to be let out.

Traffic along the road increased. He was always led across the road when he was going to help in the apple orchard on the other side. He wasn't much use. For the most part he walked around raking, and often he would rake under a single tree until the ground was all torn up and some laughing foreman came and moved him.

He had a profound horror of the motorized cultivator that arrived in 1956: one of the regular gardeners had got his foot caught that spring, and it looked awful: toes hanging loose, blood flowing, but that wasn't what frightened him. It was the helpless cry when everyone came running. After that, he refused to stay in the orchard when the cultivator got going and rushed back to the Home, across the road. They let him be.

He didn't want to hear that cry again.

He had another peculiarity which amused the men in the market garden: he was afraid of birds.

Not birds flying, not flights of wild geese and cranes and swifts tumbling high in the air in the summer evenings.

It was birds that flew up suddenly out of bushes that frightened him, sparrows fluttering up from a new-plowed field would make him beside himself with terror. Even after he had turned thirty, he would still, in spite of all prohibitions, run into the kitchen, babbling incomprehensibly.

Good-natured aides would try to comfort him with a piece of coffee-cake: he could sit for a long time, trembling and stiff, until his terror slowly wore off.

He had no words for the world, and birds' suddenly flying up was one of the thousand ways in which the world would turn *unreliable.*

The bird wasn't something that fluttered through the world, the bird was a corner of the cloth of the world which had worked loose and started to flutter.

Of course there was terror in it, but also liberation: the dream he was dreaming would have an ending.

At the end of the '50s, his parents died. Nobody tried to explain it to him, and he didn't know in what order they died or when, but when he hadn't seen them for a few years—his mother would visit him regularly twice a year and always brought him candy and apples, an anxious lot of apples, as if the lack of apples were his problem—he started to miss them, in some vague fashion, about the way you might all of a sudden long for mustard or honey or a certain kind of floury gravy with just a taste of burned pork.

He remembered the buildings better than he did his parents— the horse, the woodshed—the only thing left of his parents was the sound when they shut the door to the porch and stamped the snow off their boots in the winter.

But this sound was an important sound. It meant that the lamps would be lit, that the atmosphere in the room would change.

At the end of September every year, the willow herb, the evening primrose, has no more flowers left, but its seed pods ride on the wind, and if they get into a yard, they respond to even the slightest changes in temperature by rising and falling rhythmically. And at last they settle down, in small, quick drafts, which the wind can easily carry off again.

That was the way September was that year, in 1977.

He was sitting in the dayroom in the new Home, sixty miles from the old one, which had been torn down in 1963.

He had his favorite spot by the window. Here was an asphalt yard, without trees, without flowers, only a wilted flowerbed edging the drive and the three parking places.

Here the seeds of the willow herb came drifting in. It was the kind of September day when the air is *quite still and waiting*.

He was shapeless in his lounger; he swelled over its edges. For ten years he had been quite empty.

The drifting seed pods, unbelievably light, moved on winds so slight that no one could discern them.

Slowly the shadow of the curtain moved across the polished floor of the dayroom.

The hourglass-shaped ribbon of light moved across the surface of the planet, dawn line and dusk line rushing forward like great wings across distant plains and mountains. Slowly or swiftly, depending on how you chose to measure it, the earth moved in its orbit and would never return to the same point where it had once been. Slowly or swiftly, the solar system moved in its orbit, and with silent, dizzying speed; like a disk of light, the galaxy moved in its mysterious rotation around itself.

In the wombs of the mothers, unborn embryos were growing, membranes and tissues folded and pleated themselves cleverly around each other, exploring without sorrow, without hesitation, the possibilities of topological space.

Of this he knew nothing: heavy and huge like a boulder in the woods, he sat in his chair, moving it with effort a few inches every hour so that it always remained in the patch of sun.

He was as slow as the galaxy and as mysterious.

In the shadows of the leaves which moved more and more insistently against the wall, he saw the old mushrooms growing once more, from the first soft mound shooting up through the moss to the last black-brown pyramid of shapeless, pungent tissue in December.

For years, he allowed them to grow freely as he sat there; he made them more and more remarkable, more and more fantastic; each and every one the only one of its kind, saw them live and die; knew since long ago that all time and everything that grew were as mysterious and great as he was himself.

A Water Story

One afternoon during the cold, rainy, summer of 1977, I left Lake Åmänningen with my son Joen in a white-painted but by that time rather leaky motorboat. We went by Flodhäll, through Virsbo Lock, where the trailer trucks rumble across the bridge and the children swim happily by the sluice basin, then through Lake Virsbo, which is long and shallow, into the swampy delta country between Virsbo and Seglingsberg, where twelve wild geese flew up in front of our bow and a wonderful pair of cranes crossed our route, passed Bo Rocks, where fishermen sat so close to one another that they obscured the red paint spot which is a landmark on the starboard side of the Canal; they've been sitting like that for hundreds of years with their fishing rods, where the channel is narrowest and the current runs deep, and the skippers of oreboats and barges have cursed them as we did when, at the last second, we realized that we were on our way into what lies between the two outer rocks; but all went well, and we continued through the Seglingsberg and Fårmansbo locks, noticing that Fårmansbo has acquired a fat, handsome woman lock keeper with a Finnish accent and a huge cat and a small child playing by the water, carefully protected from falling into the deep changing element by a wooden playpen; through the last bends of the river, we arrived at dusk on North Nadden, my childhood lake.

"It's so small," said Joen, who has always heard it described as large, and I, who had started to feel chilly in the dusk and was just struck by the thought that we had a long way back, about eighteen miles, or sixty feet up to the surface of Lake Åmänningen

(and that during a summer when the lock keeper in Virsbo closed for the night at seven),

I, poor confused daddy in faded jeans and bare feet, who got cold from hours in the tea-brown humus water that continually leaked in from somewhere in the stern,

I suddenly discovered how right he was. How closed in, how melancholy was my childhood lake, with its slowly deteriorating sawmill to the north, its deforested area, barely concealed by so-called shore trees to the west, where the new road was put in quite some time ago, with the little idyllic summer houses in Brattheden to the east. The only thing that has stayed the same, relatively speaking, is the swampland to the north, the watery labyrinths of reeds and red water lilies, where you can still hear cranes occasionally.

It was that small, that closed in. Almost like a childhood in a washtub!

And while we filled up with gas from the five-liter gas can through the old blue funnel that disappeared in the spring storms in '74 and was found again among the nettles in Kyrkviken in June of '77, a faithful-retainer funnel, an honorable funnel, it occurred to me to start telling him:

"You only see a small, melancholy lake that's getting overgrown. You see a sawmill that's falling into ruin, and you see some silly little summer houses on a ridge. Most of it grown over.

"You have to understand that I see something different. In my childhood, there were lots of people here. College students in white suits and white caps gingerly rowing young girls among the reeds, conversing with them shyly. The trains come into the station, puffing coal smoke, dropping off swarms of passengers from Stockholm, my eccentric uncles and aunts among them—"

"A good half of them only exist in your novels," says Joen, who has just entered puberty and is starting to talk back.

"—I see old workingmen sitting on their porches at dusk," I continue easily, "scratching out their pipes with a nail and telling stories of fathers and forefathers, stories so old that they go back to the eighteenth century, stories about coal burners' huts and foundry owners who are so evil that the Devil himself comes to get them on Christmas Eve, and stories of the big, mysterious fish, the Giant Catfish in Bo Basin, the Great Fish, the Primordial Fish who hides in the depths where the sunlight only penetrates like a star among all the others, the Inexorable Fish who cuts off all the lead-lines with one snap of his giant teeth, so that rope and chain come up to the surface neatly cut . . ."

"—Why," said Joen, who is a modern young man who does not approve of long stories; he's in a hurry to get to the end, as if the end would be something remarkable in itself,

"—Why," said Joen, "what's he hiding, anyway?"

"—There's gold down there in the depths; far down something unbelievably rich is glistening; the darkness possesses something, and the Catfish is the Monster who protects it and hides it. Never, never will any living creature bring the gold to the surface. The monster would rather die than give up his gold. Rather die than show himself.

"As distinct from those vulgar lake monsters we read about in the papers, the Loch Ness Monster, the Great Sea Beast, and whatever they are called, the Giant Catfish in Bo Basin is a lake monster whose whole existence consists of never showing himself."

We'd hardly finished filling up before we turned north again among darkening reeds.

We rushed a bit, since we were about to miss the closing time at the locks. Joen steered through the increasingly abstract landscape while I bailed.

Frightened ducks flew by the bow; a hawk stood almost still over the forest's edge, but no cranes this time. The lock house at Fårmansbo shone yellow, friendly, inviting. Exercising all our charm, we managed to borrow the lock key. It was already so dark that the white water down there looked luminous; agitated bats whirred across the sluice basin.

It was the beginning of August; the summer light was beating a retreat.

"I often ran around here as a child, or boy, along the edge, fishing," I said. "There's some species of morels that you don't find anywhere else around here, small black ones. They're only

106

edible after you parboil them. They grow in the old slag piles. Once there was a hut there."

We got out on Lake Åmänningen again at the last moment. The canal in back of us started getting dark, but in front of us we had the large lake which reflected the evening light. Everything was very still. Our wake spread out like a theorem in a perfect geometry, an occasional grebe dived in front of us, abruptly, as if it had had second thoughts.

Outside Dentist's Point—a desolate wooded spot which got that name because the man who once built a summer house there was a dentist—with the islet called Gärholmen closest to it, we noticed something peculiar, which made Joen slow the engine to idle.

A canoe was leaving Gärholmen, evidently with a single person in it. It passed between the hazardous, sharp rocks at Enträ as if they didn't even exist and made a swift turn toward Kyrkviken.

It was so far away that it was impossible to see who was paddling it, but the way he was paddling was somehow upsetting: hectic.

"Who on earth could that be," I said.

"That's odd," Joen said. "Let's go in to Gärholmen and have a look. I have a feeling that something strange may have happened."

"It's so dark," I said.

"But I still want to put in at Gärholmen. Anyway, I hid some one-kroner pieces under a rock in the middle of the island when we were out doing long distance skating in February of '76."

He still had the small boy's mania for hiding things under rocks, especially on islands, perhaps to make himself invulnerable, perhaps to leave something invulnerable behind, perhaps just to create a secret for himself.

We approached the island at half throttle. It's quite small, a narrow islet. There are such a number of sharp, wicked rocks in the water around it that I hardly ever put in there by boat. On the other hand, it makes an excellent stopping place in the winter, the first few days after Christmas when the ice is safe and lies there blue-black because no snow has fallen yet.

By now it was almost dark. Just as we started getting in among the really dangerous shoals, simultaneously we caught sight of something that had to be a swimming animal, perhaps an elk, on its way from the island in the direction of Kyrkviken. The same direction the canoe had taken.

I made a careful ninety-degree turn. While Joen kept a lookout for the dark brown boulders that might rise to the surface at any moment, unreal, only becoming tangible the moment they touch the bow, I stood up and scouted ahead.

It was too small to be an elk, it was too large to be a swimming snake.

Thirty yards off, we realized that it was a man. He had darkish hair with a few gray strands; the hair was plastered across a rather small head, determinedly but rather slowly making its way toward shore. He seemed to be completely naked.

Were we disturbing him?

He was rather low in the water. It seemed he was swimming more and more slowly, in a determined way.

He should have seen us by now.

I made up my mind. We had hardly reached him before I realized that the man was exhausted.

We pulled him on board as well as we could. Everyone who has done this sort of thing knows that it isn't an easy matter.

A man you pull up over the stern of a motorboat and who hardly makes any effort himself easily gets his chest scraped.

We put him in the bottom of the boat, toward the bow, and pulled my wool sweater over him.

"How are you doing?" I asked.

He seemed too exhausted to be able to reply.

"What are we going to do with him?" Joen asked.

"We'll bring him back home with us," I said.

"He's very cold," Joen said. "Let's take him to Gärholmen and make a fire."

Sure enough, on Gärholmen we found a tent, an LPG stove in front of the tent, some clothes hung to dry across a low fir branch.

We put as many clothes as we could on him and made a fire with the dry sticks heaped far in under the spruces next to the tent.

The first thing he said when he could speak again was something rather surprising to us.

"Not to worry. She'll come back. She always comes back."

"O.K.," I said. "But then it might have been overdoing it a bit trying to swim after her all the way to Kyrkviken. The water turns cold faster than you like to think, here in Västmanland. And if you aren't an experienced long-distance swimmer, it makes sense to take it easy."

He didn't seem to be listening. He might have been between thirty-five and forty, a rather attractive face, commonplace as well. You might guess at some intellectual occupation, but in that case not one that would confer status. A line across his nose indicated that he normally wore glasses; I guess the thin-rimmed variety. He was still shivering and crept closer to the fire.

Actually, there was nothing to indicate that he was particularly mad or even desperate. He didn't even seem unhappy, just cold.

Consequently, I went down to the shore to see how we had disposed the boat in our haste; I had a strong feeling that the wind had changed.

It had, too: the boat was knocking against the rocks, and I took the opportunity to pull it over into the shelter of a large boulder at the edge of the shore. Now it was so dark that the closest trees were illuminated by the fire in front of the tent.

I could see some feminine underwear on a clothesline. The two figures, my son and the strange man, now had bent closer to the fire.

When I got closer, I realized that they had started to heat water.

"I thought I might make you some coffee by way of thanking you for your help," the man said. "Just instant, of course."

There was a short silence. Nobody had anything to say right then. In the silence, I felt that I was out of breath: everything had happened so fast. Also I was damn cold and hungry.

"You wouldn't have some bread and butter," I said. "You see, we've been going up and down the canal all afternoon."

"Sure thing," the swimmer said. "I even think I might have some excellent Finnish juniper-smoked sausage from Arvid Nordquist."

Bread and sausage appeared. I have to admit that we helped ourselves without restraint.

"So you're from Stockholm," I said.

"I was born around here," he said. "A bit further down the canal, that is, just above Kolbäck. My father had a farm there. I went to school in Västerås. What year did you graduate?"

"Fifty-five," I said.

"I was a bit earlier," he said. "I graduated in 1950. Then I taught for a while, but that was no good. It was the worst years in the beginning of the '60s; there wasn't a chance of maintaining discipline. Since then, I've been in the travel business. I was assigned to Athens quite a while, as the local representative of charter agency. I've been back in Stockholm seven years now."

He paused again. I tried in vain to get my wet matches to light.

"It's amazing how you can get tangled up in your life," he said.

"What do you mean?" I said.

"This girl I met for the first time in Stockholm toward the end of the '50s," he said. "It must have been 1959, something like that. I remember that the National Museum had just started their series of summer night concerts; right after we met, we went to one of those concerts. The summer of 1959 was very warm and dry, if I remember correctly. There were still quite a few streetcar lines in the city.

"We came out from the summer night concert and the city was warm, abandoned, empty in some surprising way. There were just the two of us.

"We took a streetcar to Söder; we walked along Söder Mälarstrand for a long time. I remember the wonderful elder in Skinnarvik Park, above Heleneborgsgatan. It was in bloom and had a very strong scent.

"We must have been terribly happy."

"Where did you meet originally?"

"That's not important," he said, almost offended by my inter-

110

ruption. "I think it was in a seminar at the university. I really can't remember any longer. I have the feeling that I've known her forever. She was a rather shy, slender little girl in those days. Intelligent, but shy. She was rather afraid of speaking up in the seminar. I was shy, too. I'd gone to bed with girls before her, I guess, but she was the first one I had the feeling that I *possessed*; she belonged to me, I could do what I wanted with her. Do you know what I mean?"

I nodded.

"There was something strange between us; a kind of fire, poison perhaps, like toadstool poison, muscarine, like the bog myrtle on the big bogs around Märrsjön. When we were together it was like entering a different world.

"I had a room on Hornsgatan that summer. I was supposed to study for one of the big history comprehensive exams. I didn't do that much studying. We'd often lock ourselves in for days on end, we nestled in each other like creatures on the bottom of a deep lake. What I mean to say is that reality above was no more than the glimmer of light that creatures in a lake like that would see above them, a glimmer of light through dark brown, humus-rich water.

"Like I said, both of us were shy to start with. I don't think I knew much about how to satisfy a woman in those days. I remember wondering why she had such a hard time getting to sleep now and then. Of course it didn't take very long for the shyness to wear off. She had marvelous orgasms; they would go up to her shoulders, practically. A kind of cramp that shook her whole body."

"Think of the young man," I said.

"Not to worry. He's gone to sleep. I'll get another sweater to put over him. You don't have to leave yet, do you? He could stand to get some rest after a long trip like that, right? You see—it feels a little lonely right now. And strictly speaking, you're my only connection with the mainland."

"O.K.," I said. "The boy gets to sleep for a while."

"We shared depressions, too. A kind of strange, white melan-

111

choly, the two of us. I think it has to be that way in such circumstances. I might go out into the city around eleven, walk carefully down Hornsgatan; I say carefully, because in our condition we often had the feeling that we were walking on glass all the way. It's a bit difficult to explain—well, we'd walk down Hornsgatan with the firm intention of buying food for lunch and come back with some flatbread and cheese.

"It was a terribly odd state. Like some great, metaphysical absent-mindedness, a feeling that the whole world was completely meaningless really, and that we were the only ones to have discovered it.

"Do you understand? Not the usual feeling that what you're *doing* is meaningless, but a much larger feeling: existence as a whole had lost its meaning; you had passed through all the stages that it was possible to pass through. *And there was nothing there, either.*

"Our friends started wondering what had become of us. I suspect that at the university they'd given up on us. All of this was a short time, just a few months, and quite mad. And at bottom, we always had the feeling that this wasn't going to last very long.

"We made some attempt to work together. It wasn't that easy. I only had one room and a kitchen, and between the room and kitchen such bizarre tensions developed that the walls creaked when we tried to keep away from each other so that we could at least read a book for three or four hours.

"By fall, we both realized it was dangerous. You couldn't intensify it further. There was no real road back, I mean back to the level where you have ordinary conversations with each other.

"I remember the morning she left quite well. I had packed up her things for her; she couldn't do it. The breakup paralyzed her: it was as if she'd realized something important at the last minute, something quite different, that remained to be done.

"For some reason, God knows why, perhaps she had a lot to carry—some luggage had accumulated during two and a half months—we had ordered a cab, and I was standing in the window waiting for it to drive up.

112

"Why didn't I stand down there, why didn't I say goodbye to her down in the street? You know, that's the kind of thing that's impossible to remember after so many years. One reason might be that we'd had a stupendous fight, but that doesn't have to be it. It might have been some kind of agreement.

"I must have gone into my room for a moment, I remember that. Anyway, I discovered that she had left something there, her umbrella, her little red umbrella. I remember shouting through the window, 'Do you want me to bring it down?' And she answered, 'Just throw it down.'

"There are goodbyes like that, believe it or not."

"I believe it," I said.

"Have you ever noticed an oddity about the topographical map of Västmanland," he said, and I wasn't actually surprised any longer.

"No, what do you mean?"

He went into the tent and fetched a small map, Västerås NV, as it's called, scale 1 : 50,000.

"Well, almost every one of those small lakes has an insignificant twin that is a bog: just look here, Acktjärn, and then Acktjärn Bog right next to it; Big Grillsjön, and then Grillsjön Bog like a shadow of the lake to the north. All over the place, you find a humble shadow of the lake, a bog. If you like, it's the lake that was once upon a time, a bigger lake that was there.

"But the bog is still there. Under the bog-myrtle and the meadowsweet, the cottongrass and the tussocks of cloudberries, there is still water, although it no longer reflects the sky as the lake does.

"It's still there. And then? What happens under the surface? What does a lake turned bog reflect?"

"Itself?"

"Or a different sky. A sky of peat? Have you thought about the mushrooms, how different they are from the phanerogams. Much closer to the earth, much more—how shall I put it—dramatic in their whole demeanor, with all those strange poisons, their way of growing, lightning-fast in the space of a few nights. And their way of dying, a kind of dissolution from inside. They look quite whole long after they've died."

"Don't forget that they leave filaments in the earth that go on making new mushroom bodies. Mycelium. We hardly ever see the most interesting thing about mushrooms. The underground filaments."

"I have thought about it."

"And how about you? Are you living or dead?"

"She disappeared over the horizon. I'd see her now and then, sometimes with somebody, sometimes alone. Then she married an expert of some kind, God knows what kind, and went to the U.S.

"I think we exchanged a few letters, and I remember them as rather unimportant.

"I got myself back to the point at which I'd been interrupted, so to speak. I think it was damn smart of me, that time.

"I married, a nice girl, had kids. By the way, now she's married to a forestry agent around here. It was more that she lost interest in me than the other way around. It was about the same time, by the way, that I left teaching.

"Well, then came the time in Athens. That was rather fun.

"You know, a branch office like that is the right place to get to know the country, and, I'd like to add, the right place to learn business dealings with Greeks. Their game rules are a bit different from ours; it costs you something to learn their system, and when you know both systems, it's possible to do some entertaining things.

"The risk of a situation like that, of course, is that you live rather too well. You drink a fair amount. You have a good time. You get flabby in different ways.

"You get like the steamship agents on the little islands out in the Aegean, little kings who rule the district from some café or other, standing behind some modest counter, letting the workers polish the brass while they ponder freights and real-estate prices and cement transports.

"Suddenly it can get all empty. You see, the worst thing I know is emptiness.

"You know, suddenly a dry paper will rustle along the street in the stubborn August wind, an old newspaper that someone has dropped or thrown away. In southern countries where everything is dry, where everything stays put, it's somehow more obvious than in northern countries. The summer wind rustles in the plane trees. You look up for a moment and get all scared by your own emptiness; you ask yourself what you're doing, actually.

"You know what I mean?"

He asked this last question with such eagerness, almost obstinacy, that I became uneasy. Even the boy started in his sleep. I started thinking seriously about waking him up and going home.

Then it struck me how childish this impulse to flee was, how strongly dictated by my own weaknesses, and I said:

"Of course I know what you mean. Sometimes I tell myself that it's in those moments that we look truth in the face."

"What do you mean?"

"Suppose it's that kind of emptiness that's the truth about this world? Take this lake, for instance. Certain days when I feel sad, I walk down to the shore. The rocks are out there, huge, heavy, each one a statement that cannot be refuted. Times like that, I see that the lake has always been sad. The natural world is like that. We're the only ones who try to create meaning."

There was silence for a while. Then he suddenly continued his story.

"I don't think I'd given her a thought for the last ten years. Then one day she comes into my office in Athens. She wanted to change her ticket. I was in the back room and heard one of my assistants having a bit of an argument with her out there; he tried to explain that if you're on a charter trip, you can't just change your ticket.

"I was on the phone, I think I was talking to Stockholm, and all of a sudden I hear her voice out there. It's rather a husky voice, always a bit drawling. It's hard to mistake that voice.

"I went out like a sleepwalker, and there she was. She was obviously married—at least she was wearing a wedding ring—and obviously she was there with some guy other than the one she was married to. I changed their tickets right away. They wanted to stay another week. They wanted to go to Poros. I told them it isn't easy to find a hotel on Poros right in the middle of the Greek Easter. I asked for their hotel in Athens so that I could call them. The guy seemed totally negligible to me, just a nice-looking clod.

"I had time to ask her how she was. 'Fine,' she said, 'as you can see.'

"'That's good,' I said. 'Too bad we won't have time for a drink. We could walk down to Syntagma and have some coffee.'

"'We won't have time,' she said. 'We've promised to meet some friends at four.'

"'Too bad, after all these years,' I said.

"I was the last one to leave the office, as usual, going through a few things I'd always go through. Telexes, lists of things to do, orders. I had promised to play tennis with a guy who used to play on the courts up by the university. I remember thinking that I'd just get a sandwich first and that I might as well wait until the worst traffic was over.

"Then there's a knock on the door. I go over and open up. It's the doorkeeper in the building.

"'There's a lady here looking for you who's very insistent,' he said. 'I've told her that you close at four and that she should come back tomorrow. But nothing helps. She just pushes in. Do you know her?'

"'Not really,' I said.

"I heard the clock ticking. I looked at the teletype, still and silent under its dust cover. I looked at the typewriters. Oh yes, I remember thinking: So there are moments that can decide your whole life."

"And then?"

"And then I went and opened up. It was like opening a sluice gate.

"We went to her hotel and got her stuff. It was a little awkward to move her into my apartment, since I had a Greek girlfriend living there. We borrowed an apartment from a friend for a couple of days.

116

"Well," he said, "if she didn't take the train she should be here pretty soon."

"Does she often take off like that?" I asked.

"Sometimes she feels she can't stand it. Me, too. Quite honestly, it's rather trying to be as terribly dependent on each other as we are. Sometimes she runs off, sometimes I do."

"There is a desire for solitude," I said, rather stupidly. "I mean" (and I think I increased my stupidity by that remark) "there is even a desire for unhappiness."

"I still don't think you've quite grasped it," he said.

"In a way, I think we're living in different worlds," I said.

I thought that was a polite way of getting away from it.

When the boy woke up, he stretched his arms in the air and yawned loudly. It took a while for him to grasp where he was. He went behind some bushes to take a leak, and he was gone longer than expected.

At the same time, a canoe came into the inlet, just beside my boat. It appeared almost ghostlike out of the August darkness.

I was already down by the shore.

I said a polite hello. She was shorter than I'd imagined. Not really beautiful, actually. She treated me with polite indifference.

Then the boy came at last. We said goodbye and pushed the boat out.

It took us quite a while to get the old Archimedes E 4 going.

In the intervals, while I pulled on the starter cord, Joen sat jingling something in his right hand.

"What's that you're jingling?" I asked.

"The coins of course. The one-kroner pieces I hid under the rock last winter, when we took a break when we were out skating. I've got them now."

I often wonder in how many places on the lake he hides such coins.

117

The Bird in the Breast

Suddenly it was summer again, and she looked around the room, unable to recognize a single piece of furniture. Instead there was a chestnut tree outside the window, a tree that had just shed its blossoms and which hadn't been there a few days ago. As she woke up in the brief, dry, hard manner of very old people, she indolently registered a memory of having moved from the Old People's Home in Kolbäck to the Long-Term Care Facility in Köping.

Her relatives would pick up the furniture later; it wasn't easy to reach them, for as usual at this time of year, they were at their summer cottage up in the northern part of the district.

She seemed to remember that she had once been fond of her inlaid chest of drawers. There had been a crystal vase with a gilt glass lid, a candy dish, where her mother had kept sweets. You were not allowed to touch it without permission; it could easily get broken.

She hoped her relatives wouldn't break it now that they were taking care of her things. Her mother might get mad.

The new furniture was white, very impersonal, consisting of a bedside table and a chest of drawers; there was furniture just like it across the room, where apparently another patient was asleep. She glimpsed a very thin body under the waffle-patterned hospital blanket. It seemed to be sleeping.

A faint but penetrating smell of urine seemed to fill the building where she was to live now for the rest of her life. It came from the corridor where the sound of wheeled trays, rustling across vinyl floors, was interrupted by the clatter of metal dishes and the nurses' girlish voices with singsong Finnish accents.

Everything was as it should be. This was the place where she lived now.

She turned toward the depths again, sank through deep, clear

118

water where only some water plants were pulled out by the current like the long tresses of a woman's hair.

In just a few seconds, she covered immense distances. Now she was down in the starless darkness where the real struggle was going on. She didn't know anything about this darkness except that it was a darkness. It was close by or far off, whichever you liked.

The Prisoner had many shapes. It was by his gaze that you could recognize him.

The first time she recognized his gaze was when she was twelve, sitting on the back steps of her father's house in Västmanland, a small girl with a book.

That time he had been a viper who suddenly lay there, sunning himself on the tar-brown planks two yards from her feet.

That he was a viper wasn't the important part. The important part was the gaze in his narrow, yellow eyes. It betrayed him. The blackness in the narrow slits of his eyes was the same as the darkness between galaxies.

She had always said no, and this no was the one skill of her life.

When her sisters and brothers flocked past with berry baskets and sunhats, Papa in the lead with his walking stick, there were many years when they kept trying to get her to come along with them. "Fredrika, come, there are so many blueberries to pick in the woods! Fredrika, the weather's so beautiful!"

On clear days, you could hear their voices all the way to the farmhouse farthest along the road. As the years went by, the obligatory question to Fredrika turned into a ritual; nobody expected her actually to join them.

Then it was the end of the 1890s; Papa was still quite strong and ruddy, Mama thinner, paler. The grocery store was at the bend in the road, right where the brook passed under the road through a culvert of heavy, cut rocks. There was no gas pump in the yard— when did the gas pump get there? The large alders along the brook provided deep shadow. She remembered clearly how you could see the seaweed, the long, narrow leaves of seaweed, pulled out by the current like a woman's hair.

She remembered the wheels of the horse-drawn carriages, the

metal clangor of the iron-clad carriage wheels which changed their note as they passed over the old, worn planks of the bridge. When the farmers came to do their shopping, you heard them from far off.

The suppliers' laughter coming from Papa's office, the Butcher, the Wholesaler, the Ironmonger from Köping, and the Metalsmith who was a cousin and who had strange, large sideburns which had amused her when she was a child.

The singing in the Mission House, the flag that was flown on the King's Name Day, the first birds of spring.

She had been married off to the Butcher, who was a bit older but still a young man. He had very thin eyebrows of blond hair across light, watery eyes, big cheeks that made his head look like a pear.

He looked at her with large, watery eyes when she weighed out tacks for him and folded the bag over, big, human, pale eyes a bit red around the rims, eyes that wanted something from her.

She didn't want to. Saying no was her skill.

Papa died the fall after the wedding, her brothers and sisters moved into town, Mama wasn't well, there were whispers about bankruptcy. The Butcher had three rooms above the shop. She had got new curtains.

Her way of saying no was very easy. She simply absented herself. She wasn't there. What was there was a body, and a body was something else. Anybody might penetrate another body.

During the fall, his manner toward her changed. He smelled of liquor in the mornings too, but just a little.

The first snow came, and she wiped off the oilcloth on the kitchen table and heard the heavy thumps of meat being cut up on a butcher block on the floor below her.

Sound traveled well; it was an old wooden house with very little insulating sawdust in the flooring. When he necked with the new girl in the shop, she heard that, too.

It didn't touch her.

Once and for all, it was a fact that she didn't belong in the ordinary world; it wasn't hers, and that was the way it was going to be.

Already as a small child she experienced it, when she heard her parents and her brothers and sisters speak to each other.

She was a quick child: it wasn't that she had any difficulty learning the words.

She spoke just as clearly as her brothers and sisters, perhaps a little more softly, that was all.

But the words weren't hers. She had no right to them.

"What beautiful weather we've got today, little Fredrika," her father might say. And she knew that meant the sunshine, the flag flapping in the faint southwest breeze, the tufts of cloud in the sky, yes, she knew exactly what he meant, of course she did, she wasn't stupid.

But she was quite convinced that there was something else behind what he said, some remainder, a secret that she'd never reach.

She once tried discussing it with Karl, who was the quietest of her brothers. "Does everybody mean the same thing when they speak of 'a red color,' or do different people see different kinds of red and still use the same color word for different colors? Do you think that might be the way of it?"

But Karl didn't understand her. She never succeeded in expressing herself so as to make herself intelligible.

The second winter, the Butcher started to beat her. It did not come as a surprise. For a long time, he'd been calling her "Trash," addressing her in the third person plain and simple, heaping violent abuse on the potatoes, which had burned. He got red spots above his light blond eyebrows when he was furious.

The fleshly part was over. (She always connected "desires of the flesh" with the meat in the butcher shop; it all made a bloody, revolting entity.) He no longer tried to penetrate her absent body with his large, blushing member which, close up, looked like a blind head with a mouth (but a mouth placed vertically and not horizonally like all other mouths in hungry nature)—she became acquainted with other kinds of pain.

She discovered that getting kicked in the shins hurt more than getting slapped in the face, that your shins ache for much longer afterward. She discovered that a wound in the forehead allows the

121

blood to run down toward the eyes, where it stings. She learned that if someone holds your wrist in a hard, firm grip, it isn't as easy to get loose as you might think.

She learned to be quiet, to watch for the storm that was coming, to see it well in advance and disappear in her black shawl out into the snowy road on a lonely walk which might be long because you never quite knew when it would be safe to walk back home again.

The wind polished the crusty snow, white swirls in front of her feet, and she was there, as much in the swirls as in her thin, freezing body.

It still wasn't hers, as little as the world she'd been submerged in was hers.

Her brothers and sisters never came to visit. She hid from people, showed herself in daylight more and more seldom, had a feeling that people in the community were pointing their fingers at her.

The second winter, she was very quiet. She wanted to become one with the shadows, make herself invisible. It was an effort to move about in rooms where someone might suddenly knock on the door, come in, and shake your head on its thin neck so that it hit the doorpost.

In February of that year, the Butcher hanged himself on one of his own meathooks. It was right during the first big February snowstorm, and it took a long time for the sheriff and the county doctor to get there.

She called them up herself on the newly installed telephone and told them in a clear, girlish, fluting voice what had happened.

While she was waiting for the doctor, she cut the Butcher down with one of the long, ground-down knives in the shop and sat there with his heavy body in her lap. It didn't frighten her any longer: it was a heavy doll, very pale with very blond eyebrows. That a rag doll could be so terribly heavy, that a human being could actually be such an immense weight, was beyond her imagination.

It didn't touch her much. It didn't happen in her life.

Her sister, now working as a cook on an estate down toward Strömsholm, took her in.

She was a Pentecostal. The precious blood of the Lamb, speaking in tongues, prayer sighs, and the Book of Revelation, in which seal after seal is broken over a world where the catastrophes blow up like thunderstorms across the lakes of childhood.

Her sister was calm, trusting, secure in herself. Piously, she played religious songs for male quartet on the old record player in the back room. When Lewi Pethrus became the leader of her church, she put his picture on the wall.

For Fredrika, it wasn't that easy. This Lamb wanted something from her, it made demands on her which she wasn't up to.

She was outside this, too. She felt that everything the mild young pastors with their slicked-down hair, soft voices, and pious blue eyes witnessed about was intended for the others, that as well as everything else.

They spoke with a lot of passion about the desires of the flesh, about the Powers of Darkness; they spoke of sins as if there were many. And it was fundamentally incomprehensible to her, since she clearly saw that there was only one, and that one irremediable.

Creation was evil. And in some strange way, the others were incapable of seeing that.

Evil gall wasps laid their eggs in the paralyzed larvae of other insects who, still sentient, allowed themselves to be devoured from the inside. Cancer cells groping their way into living tissue with their long, narrow, hairlike fingers. Deer hunted to death by dogs on crusty snow.

Decades passed, and the Prisoner didn't make a sign, didn't appear. Still she knew he was there, that he knew all her movements and thoughts.

What they had in common was a No.

He turned up again at a Pentecostal meeting the same night as the Germans invaded Norway: April 9, 1940. It was a very violent meeting, with much speaking in tongues, much talking about the Last Day and the seal that would be broken and Armageddon, which was close, prayer sighs and cries. The meeting took place in the recently built Elim Church on Köpingsvägen in Västerås; outside the windows, a light April rain fell on the still bare trees.

There was much talk of the Powers of Darkness, and this confused and disturbed her; for her, darkness had always meant something good.

Suddenly the Prisoner was there. He had the head of an aurochs, or perhaps an insect, the yellow eyes of an aurochs, and in his narrow eye slits a darkness which was the cold, quiet darkness between the stars. He didn't speak: he was just there in front of her, implacable, with the clarity of a constellation in the sky.

But later, after a stay in a psychiatric clinic where she was being cared for because she spoke in a disjointed manner and seemed to be haunted by visions and was treated with health food cereals and long walks, she is supposed to have confided to her sister that he had said, "Fredrika, your time will come. Your time will come. Your time will come when I enter into my power."

With the passing of the years, she became more and more disoriented. It was hard to understand what she was talking about. Her sister sent her down to the cellar to get a jar of jam, since her own weak knees had given out. When she didn't come back up in an hour, the sister made herself go down on aching and recalcitrant knees and found her down there, sitting on the potato box, incessantly and monotonously speaking into one of the dark corners.

She was a cross. She wasn't much use.

The first few days and nights in the Long-Term Care Facility were hot. The other woman always seemed to be asleep; reluctantly, she allowed herself to be fed a couple of times a day. That was all.

Outside the main entrance a car braked; you heard the sound of bottles and of glass, and the driver talking to his assistant about something that had got lost. That was all.

After four days, it started to brew up for a thunderstorm. The barometer dropped, and she knew it without having a barometer; she recognized the signs from her childhood. She was lying in such a way that she could see the thunderclouds from a corner of her pillow. They were the same kind of heavy, rolling clouds she had seen in her childhood, thunderclouds pregnant with rain, with power, over the Västmanland fields.

And the enormous voice speaking to her through her days and her nights grew stronger and stronger.

The only way in which this speaking could be seen on the outside was from the small drops of clear, thin perspiration that glued her tendrils of white hair to her forehead, which was just as white, and from her lips, which were moving constantly.

The speech of the Prisoner was very great, very strange, and quite incomprehensible. And she pondered it all in her heart. Sometimes it was about a time older than creation, older than the Milky Way and the rotating galaxies. It was about imprisoned and betrayed creation, captured behind the terrible walls of the material world. It was about the desires of the flesh, about the dark slope of passion which prevents people from reaching the glittering water surface above, the knowledge of a freedom that once existed.

She wanted to know his name, but this wish was not granted.

The voice spoke of the Last Things, about another time, when the invisible world would inundate the visible world, when the bonds that keep everything beneath the moon in captivity would be loosed.

He taught her many things.

He taught her that a human being is not a body, that animals aren't bodies either, that they are something else, something quite different, which is imprisoned in a bodily shape.

Time was on the way to its end: history had completed its mission. With ingenious tools, humanity was on its way down to the center, down to the mysterious hearts of elementary particles, and when it arrived at the very center, it would discover something tremendous which would render all history impossible.

Humanity would realize that since the beginning of time, it had been deceived.

This enormous, solid world was nothing but appearance, an evil dream, nothing else.

125

Since the thunderstorm, the nurse had started nagging about something. It seemed to be a shot. She would always beat it off with a narrow blue-white hand, so energetically that she risked getting stung by the sharp needle. She wanted to get back to the darkness where the voice was.

The nurse stopped insisting.

It had always been her skill to say no.

On the last of the seven days after the thunderstorm, the Prisoner told her his name and all of nature fell silent around her.

After that he spoke no more. At first, the silence was overwhelming. She understood that it was the same silence that had once existed in her childhood, the silence beyond words, the secret that the others didn't want to express, the conspiracy they didn't want to betray.

Now she understood everything, and she was calm.

A few days later, or perhaps it was weeks, perhaps months, she heard the Bird in the Breast for the first time.

To begin with, it was very faint, like a flute played at a great distance on a summer evening, resounding through the landscape. It was the most wonderful melody she had ever heard. For three days it kept coming closer; it grew until it seemed to fill the whole world, like birdsong in June.

She immediately realized that she herself was playing, that she and the bird were one and the same.

It was like when a very long, very complicated game reaches its conclusion and you are somehow back at the beginning again.

She felt a strange desire simply to stand up and walk, to become a little girl sitting on the porch reading, not wanting to go with her brothers and sisters to the woods.

Everything was over now, and she could start at the beginning again, that's how it seemed to her.

Now the nurse didn't come alone, but every afternoon she was accompanied by two white-coated men, and it was no longer possible to ward off the shot, the long, sharp needle.

126

She defended herself fiercely, not her body, but the bird, the wonderful Bird in the Breast. They pushed her down with gentle and heavy force; they almost sat on her.

The bird was so strong that only after ten days had gone by did they succeed in silencing it.

Out of the Pain

The pain, which until now had had sole dominion and been its own universe, slowly rotating on its own enigmatic axis, at last started to change color from whitish green to red.

He became aware of a stubborn voice drilling and drilling inside of him, a nagging voice which went through Greek verb forms, a teacher in his old boarding school with its dark vaults, who must have died a long time ago. And now he went through the aorist forms of one Greek verb after the other; he never wanted to stop, and the terrible thing was that it was completely unnecessary.

He already knew all the Greek verbs in both the imperfect and the aorist tense.

In this world, the gray-green world where he was, there ought not to be any Greek verbs, and slowly he was reminded that once there must have been another world, one where such conditions existed.

The world of pain was full, complete, a universe where nothing could be subtracted or added. This was the most perfect of all worlds, for it contained a single characteristic, and this characteristic was spread evenly through space.

In this other world, the one which must have existed once, like the monotonous droning of an old high school teacher, like the faint movements of ivy outside the windows just before afternoon rain, like the smell of chalk and ink, like the traces of generations of penknives in desk tops of sturdy ash, like the smell of vomit from his own pillow (evidently this time it hadn't helped to put a basin next to the couch when his migraine attack started) which he found undescribably disgusting, and which at the same time reminded him that in that other world, something like himself must exist—in *this* other world, there was a sense of loss. It was less perfect.

It was toward the end of the fourth day of one of his really major migraine attacks, the ones that surpassed all understanding, and while the afternoon outside the drawn brown curtains slowly changed to evening, he gradually became aware that he must be in a room in a pension—one of the cheaper pensions—on the shore of Lago Maggiore where the cheap hotels were, east of Lugano, and the wallpaper, which was very dark, had a rhomboid pattern.

The rhombs were drawn with lines that must once have been a kind of golden color but which had now turned green.

Between him and the oilcloth-covered desk, the kerosene lamp, the travel inkbottle with its safety cork, the green notebooks that he had busied himself with last week, there was now a sea. Portugal or the Cyclades could not be any harder to reach than his desk.

There wasn't much else in the room. The bed he was lying on, which you could convert into a couch in the daytime, with a pillowcase now smeared with his own greenish vomit.

The washstand with the basin he had moved temporarily close to the bed, two bulging leather trunks, worn, once elegant perhaps, with traces of careless handling by unnumerable coachmen and porters, the always well-brushed but ever more frayed overcoat on its hook by the door.

The lake was not having one of its great sunsets. As soon as dusk had fallen, quick gusts of wind—the kind that makes it so dangerous for sailors—swept across the northern part of the lake; from the vicinity of Brissago, the sound of thunder.

The raindrops beat against the window like the children's hands.

Every time he tried to open his eyes, he could see a little more clearly. And—something that was a still better sign—his double vision had almost completely disappeared. It seemed that this was the end of one of his really big, totally devastating migraine attacks. However, he could not discount the possibility that it was simply a pause, a lull in the storm, morbidly still water in the eye of the tropical storm, where, in principle, he might be able to stay for twenty-four hours, hardly longer.

This sort of thing had happened before: he had started hoping too soon.

Right in the eye of the storm, in these lulls between the pain that seared his head with white heat and this terrible nausea, which continued day in and day out, long after his stomach was emptied of its thin contents, here in the middle of the lull there was knowledge to be had, strange, almost *yellowish* knowledge (in this condition even the most abstract phenomena had colors).

It might be about words, about how *the words* turned into narrow, as it were Newtonian rings in all the colors of the rainbow, gliding swiftly across the not completely pure surface into very deep and dark water. When the words collided with each other, they could either repel each other or attract each other, forming long molecular chains.

Until the chain became too heavy, or too pretentious, and then it would break again.

It might be about *history*, about events, about monarchs, about war, about crowds of people moving restlessly through the narrow, stepped alleys of Oriental cities, about speakers in town squares, where sharp sunlight made the shadows fall hard and pitiless.

And all this, the noise in the squares, the throngs of people, the pitiless light across bent backs, assumed the shape of a rising and falling surge, the surge of sound in a large seashell.

Or the sound of the movements on the surface when, deep down in moving water, you still sense the movements of the surface, its ringing, rising, and falling sounds, like the fragments of distant music.

And this history existed. Or did not exist. Just as you liked.

He no longer remembered how many weeks there had been since he last saw blue sky.

He needed a clear sky, a great, completely spotless—no, he meant cloudless—sky in order to think clearly.

Under gray skies, the shadows threatened him.

Oh, if only he were in Sils, if it had been lovely late summer in the Upper Engadin instead of heavy November in the lowlands!

But Sils was long since covered by deep snow; all the passes were closed, and the lodges were closed. Across the green meadows up by Ley, across the paths to Val Fex, there was now only this heavy whirl of darkness and snowstorms.

And the child-hands of the rain continued to beat against the windowpane, knocking restlessly as if they really wanted to get in.

If only there had been someone!

But the single person from whom he might count on something that even remotely resembled human interest was the blonde proprietress of the pension, already past her prime, who pattered uneasily along the hallways, up- and downstairs at late hours like a restless spirit, and who, on at least one occasion, had looked in on him to "see if he was sick."

God how he detested her!

There was—in her witchlike, stooping gait, in her slovenly stockings, sagging around her ankles, in her sharp, determined nose, in her shrill voice—something which, in some awful way, reminded him of his sister.

One of those connoisseurs of souls, one of those who venture forth at dusk to stalk their prey. A word to the wise is sufficient.

At this moment, he realized that he was on his way back into the ordinary world; he was again capable of hatred, and that was enough to tell him that once again he had survived, that he had grown stronger again.

These moments when he returned he liked to imagine as a hunter's return from a long hunt in a deep, impenetrable forest. If only he knew what kind of prey he carried with him from there.

It had been the same thing for almost his entire life. It wasn't true that it had started in Basel—it was only the pain that had started

131

in Basel. He'd felt it much earlier than that, as early as Pforta—like some strange state between dream and waking, which could sneak up on him in the middle of a class, a buzzing in the deepest layer of his consciousness as if a wasp were shut up in there.

Perhaps it had started after the winter when one of his stubborn boyhood colds had turned into an ear infection and, quite obviously, penetrated the fine membranes of his brain. No one had actually taken it seriously.

Or else it might have been part of him from birth: his mother, too, had a frail, precarious constitution.

No matter: it had broken out in Basel. It had turned into fate, destiny. Perhaps it was in Basel that he had decided on it—or it had decided on him.

The dusk outside, which had never been proper day, was changing into night. For the first time in a long while he started feeling something resembling ordinary, normal sleepiness. That was always a good sign.

He started thinking about how many years it might be since he had left his professorship in Basel, the blessed professorship, along with his students, his friends, his colleagues, the friendly, ancient city with its green-shimmering roofs, its little friendly bars with windows of leaded glass and heavy oak tables, Basel with its friendly smells of beer, sausage, and ash-wood fires, Basel where so much water flows under the bridges.

Paradise, but hell at the same time. Of course, it was the pain that drove him away from there, but just as much the awareness that it wasn't his life. He calculated it must be twelve years already—twelve years of loneliness, of illness, of days and nights such that only the bravest person would dare to imagine them repeated.

Hours, and again hours, of uninterrupted nearsighted writing, his whole head bent over the table, his thick glasses only an inch above the paper; happy, ecstatic writing, while the ticking of the clocks receded and became unimportant, while mealtimes passed and were forgotten; writing like a silent, ongoing feast, where the music that slumbered at the heart of things became audible and was transformed into a note endurable to human sense.

For this mysterious music you had to be prepared to sacrifice a lot.

And so: Ariadne, faceless, or faceless in memory, deep inside the labyrinth, in memory surrounded by a music inaudible in the ordinary world. Ariadne, surrounded by nothing but her music; Ariadne, who was at once his key and his jailer.

How far in the past those secret days in Treibchen, those short trips across the big lake, how fragile those memories! And just the same, they held him captive.

Like reflections in a lake, this world multiplied continuously.

And yet he could never be sure whether this world of repetitions was the real world or he was moving among mirrors a sorcerer had arranged in his prison to ensure his calmness or docility.

Around him, outside the windows, the world darkened; the squalls over the lake took on renewed force. Around him, Europe was industrializing itself—a Europe which, with each passing year, became more unlike itself, more and more a parody, an evil repetition created by inferior gods. From the desolate autumnal fields streamed the poor of the earth, the former bond slaves of Pomerania and Mecklenburg, to fill the factories. The English cities grew like evil mushrooms under their clouds of smoke.

Old bonds and old curses were being replaced by others, heavier, unfamiliar.

Soon the smoke of the locomotives would rise toward the ceilings of the railroad stations' castiron cathedrals: oh, he knew them already. How often hadn't he seen them at night out of a dirty, steamed-up window, wrapped in his lap robe, cold as always, squeezed into a corner of the compartment, taking cover from night and loneliness.

Truly, wasn't he a Minotaur, alone in the night, alone at his own birth, forever locked into the labyrinth of this century?

From that thought there was only a very short step to the leave-taking from his friends, from the disdained, misunderstood friends, Paul Ree and Lou.

He wanted, and he didn't want, to imagine that leave-taking one last time. He had thought about it all too many times, and always with the same horrible feeling of *having made himself less than he was.*

Oh, he remembered everything as if it had happened just a few minutes ago: the leave-taking, the conversations, his sister's awful intervention, his own childish surprise *that someone was capable of abandoning him.*

And although he had thought these thoughts so many times, it was only at this moment he realized that *everything would have been perfect without him.*

The lives of his friends, the lives of his parents, this new world with its rootless proletarian masses journeying from one kind of slavery to another, from the rainy earth to the dark factories, these new smithies capable of forging the bonds of the future. And everything taking place during hopeful singing of Sankey's evangelical hymns in new houses of prayer with other rhythms than the pietistic rhythms of his childhood: the Crucified One, on his way to conquer India with cotton cloth and rob Asia of its budding industries in favor of a Christian world market, everything, from beginning to end, from the first lesson in morphology in the dark halls of Pforta, *everything would have been perfect without him.*

And—it suddenly struck him—his task was exactly that. *He was a truth.* He was the point of an incidental but very clever joke.

This leave-taking—so far back in time—whose hands still beat on the window, from Ree, from Lou, was, in spite of the continuing fever of the wound, the most beautiful thing he had experienced. So light and cheerful, and at the same time so serious and deep that he could still recall its breathing, it was a vehement reminder that life is easy, that it consists of purest lust, and that it only exists for those who are able to dance and to laugh.

134